UNDERCOVER CHRISTMAS ESCAPE

TERRI REED

LOVE INSPIRED SUSPENSE

INSPIRATIONAL ROMANCE

LOVE INSPIRED® SUSPENSE
INSPIRATIONAL ROMANCE

ISBN-13: 978-1-335-59775-5

Undercover Christmas Escape

Copyright © 2023 by Terri Reed

Love Inspired
22 Adelaide St. West, 41st Floor
Toronto, Ontario M5H 4E3, Canada
www.LoveInspired.com

Printed in U.S.A.

It was imperative they got out of the situation alive, with no fatalities. Including Sera.

The masked man faced the crowd. "Thank you for your cooperation. See, that wasn't so bad. We're not evil, just trying to make our way in the world. We'll be leaving you now. And we won't see you again." He leveled a finger at Sera. "You're coming with us."

"No!" Duncan wasn't about to let them take Sera.

"It's all right," Sera said, putting her hand on Duncan's forearm. "You'll find me."

Her words slammed into him, reminding him of the tracker in the pocket of her dress. One of Ivan's men moved to grasp Sera by the arm and tugged her toward Ivan and Angelina while a different henchman aimed his rifle at Duncan.

A riot of protective urges surged. "I'm coming, too!"

Ivan laughed. "Two hostages are plenty. And if you follow, I'll kill them."

Duncan's heart dropped. No way was he standing idly by while his partner was kidnapped.

Terri Reed's romance and romantic suspense novels have appeared on the *Publishers Weekly* top twenty-five and NPD BookScan top one hundred lists, and have been featured in *USA TODAY*, *Christian Fiction* magazine and *RT Book Reviews*. Her books have been finalists for the Romance Writers of America RITA® Award and the National Readers' Choice Award and finalists three times for the American Christian Fiction Writers Carol Award. Contact Terri at terrireed.com or PO Box 19555, Portland, OR 97224.

Books by Terri Reed

Love Inspired Suspense

Buried Mountain Secrets
Secret Mountain Hideout
Christmas Protection Detail
Secret Sabotage
Forced to Flee
Forced to Hide
Undercover Christmas Escape

Alaska K-9 Unit

Alaskan Rescue

Rocky Mountain K-9 Unit

Detection Detail

Pacific Northwest K-9 Unit

Explosive Trail

Visit the Author Profile page at LoveInspired.com for more titles.

My heart is inditing a good matter:
I speak of the things which I have made touching the king:
my tongue is the pen of a ready writer.
—*Psalm* 45:1

To Dolores, Lorna and Kim. You made high school and every reunion since fun! Reconnecting with you three has been a joy and a balm to my soul. Go Wildcats!

ONE

"This thing itches," Deputy US Marshal Seraphina Morales groused beneath her breath. Her fingers curled around the camera in her hand to keep from plucking the gray, curly-haired wig and bonnet from her head so she could scratch at her scalp. The plastered-on smile she'd adopted the moment they'd arrived at the Fleming Investments Group's Christmas party made her cheeks ache.

"Come on, Tex, you look cute." Standing a scant two feet away, DEA Agent Duncan O'Brien's distracting voice was soft and smooth as honey through the communication device lodged in her ear canal. "A glimpse into your future, eh, Sera?"

Without letting her smile slip, she slanted her fellow undercover task force member a daggered glance. Was he suggesting she'd make a cute grandmotherly type? "I could say the same about you."

Duncan patted the pillow over his tummy beneath the red velvet suit trimmed with white faux fur, and black buttons that matched his knee-high black boots. "Yeah. And I make this look good."

Sera snorted. At six feet tall, Duncan towered over

her own five-foot-five frame. His broad shoulders filled out the red velvet Santa jacket in a way she found distracting. He was the biggest Santa she'd ever seen. Most of the department-store Santas she'd come across were more her height and certainly not so well muscled. Even with the suit covering Duncan's limbs, there was no mistaking the man had a fine physique.

Even so, she was sure they resembled cartoon characters rather than Santa and Mrs. Claus.

But Sera had to admit Duncan's smiling blue eyes were mesmerizing beneath the white, bushy eyebrows attached over his own brown ones. A fake bulbous nose over his straight nose, cheeks made rosy by blush and a white beard covering his strong jaw completed the look. A handsome Santa indeed. One every woman at the party had sent a second and third glance at.

Unable to resist, she took a step closer and reached with one hand to smooth a wayward artificial curl in his fake beard. "Did you use enough spirit gum on this thing?" The classic theater costume adhesive used by actors during performances was a favorite for undercover work.

His white-gloved hand captured her bare hand. Even through the fabric, warmth radiated up her arm. A disconcerting sensation.

"Hey, now. A man's beard is a matter of pride." His deep tone resonated through her like acoustic waves.

What would his singing voice be like? Resonant and impassioned? What type of range would he have?

Snatching her hand from his, she sighed, irritated at herself for thinking of Duncan as handsome. Why on earth would she want to hear him sing? The last thing she needed in her life was to be attracted to a coworker.

Especially this one.

Shifting her focus, she glanced around the expansive space, her gaze traveling over the many well-dressed guests, ranging in ages that covered at least four decades. She noted the exits, calculated the distance to each from where she stood. It was always a good idea to have an exit strategy. Though tonight, she wasn't expecting trouble. This was purely an intel-gathering mission. Taking down their suspect would come later.

The interior lobby of the 28th floor of the prestigious Santander Tower, which was located in the heart of Dallas's historic main district, had been transformed from a professional business setting into a Christmas wonderland, reminding Sera of the impending holiday.

Her own apartment back in San Antonio remained unadorned and would remain so while she was in Dallas, assigned to this task force. But she took note of the abundance of sparkly decorations, ranging from over-the-top gaudy to vintage chic. None of which were her style. Did she even have a style? Who knew. She never saw the point in decorating when she worked through the holidays. Working was better than being home alone.

Outside the large plate glass windows lining one wall, the lights of Dallas glimmered against the dark December sky. On the platform at the far end of the brokerage's lobby, a string quartet played iconic Christmas music, soothing in its familiarity. Twinkle lights hung from the ceiling, illuminating round tables decorated with white linen tablecloths and snowflake-shaped tea lights. Laughter echoed off the rafters. Everyone seemed to be having a good time.

Though Sera couldn't prove it, she was sure the brokerage firm was laundering money for several criminal enterprises. Including Los Campeones, a moniker that when translated into English meant The Champions. Sera assumed the name was a way of letting the authorities, as well as other criminals, know they wouldn't be bested.

She'd been monitoring drug overdoses and arrests ever since the US Marshals had been instrumental in putting Tomas Garcia, the head of the Garcia cartel, behind bars. Sera had been the first to realize a new drug cartel had sprung up, led by Ramon Vega.

Vega had evaded capture and broken off from the Garcia cartel when Tomas's illegitimate daughter, Maria Montoya, had supposedly taken over. All leads on Maria had gone cold. Rumor had it she'd fled the country. Hard to know what was true when they had nothing but her name to go on.

Sera's focus had then shifted to Los Campeones. Hunting fugitives was the more exciting aspect of her job with the US Marshals Service. She excelled at identifying, locating and arresting even the most prolific of criminals.

She'd been recruited to join a newly formed task force between the marshals, DEA, ATF and FBI, and headed by Homeland Security, to find and arrest Ramon Vega.

After months of chasing down dead-end leads, the task force had finally received a tip from one of Duncan O'Brien's informants claiming Ramon and his top lieutenants would be attending the Fleming Investments Group's Christmas party scheduled for two weeks before Christmas Day—tonight.

Sera had volunteered to infiltrate the party and had pitched the idea that if she could get close to Ramon, she could put a tracker on him. Then they could follow and arrest all of Los Campeones. A win-win for the task force. They could put the new drug cartel behind bars before Christmas.

Her idea had been approved and she'd thought she would attend as a guest, but then Duncan had come up with the zany idea of the two of them posing as Santa and Mrs. Claus. The undercover disguises would allow them to capture the images of the guests by taking pictures with Santa as they entered the party.

The idea was ridiculous and brilliant at the same time. Sera could have declined and let one of the other female task force members take on the role of Mrs. Claus, padded dress and all, but she'd seen the challenge sparking in Duncan's crystal-blue gaze.

She wouldn't give him the satisfaction of seeing her back out. Though, why his opinion mattered, she couldn't say. So she'd donned the long, plumped and padded red velvet dress, and white apron with a nice pocket in which to hide the disc-shaped tracker, along with the itchy wig and bonnet. Oh, and she couldn't forget the wire-rimmed, fake glasses, which concealed a hidden camera. Ugh. Totally cartoon-worthy.

"Your hat's crooked," she told Duncan to cover the fact she'd glanced at him again.

He grinned and reached up to adjust the red hat with the large white pompom. "Yes, ma'am. You know we should take this gig on the road. Visit hospitals, shelters and churches. Hand out toys to all the children."

"You'd probably scare them," she muttered.

"No more than you."

Aware that the other team members could hear their conversation through the com links, she just bared her teeth at him.

"Do you two ever not squabble?" FBI Agent Jackie Post, a tall blonde with bright green eyes, murmured through the com link. Wearing black slacks and a white button-down shirt, she was undercover as part of the waitstaff.

"We're just making the most of the situation," Duncan quipped, saving Sera from having to answer.

The photo booth provided partygoers the opportunity to have a picture taken with Santa and was located strategically at the entrance to the festivities. Nobody would be able to bypass them without having their photo taken. Either on purpose by posing with Santa, aka Duncan, or by the tiny camera hidden in Sera's glasses. At the very least, an image would be captured by the hidden live-camera feed concealed in the elaborately scrolled top of the large Santa throne.

The plan was sound—a way to identify members of Los Campeones and Ramon, but also put faces to Fleming Investments Group's other patrons.

Because they had been unwittingly hired by Brennan Fleming's assistant to take photos of the party guests, there was no expectation of privacy. The waitstaff consisted of two other task force members who would be taking candid photos, as well.

All of the images would be instantly uploaded to a

cloud-based database that was being monitored by additional task force members, and would be run through facial recognition software.

The ding of the elevator announced more guests.

"Here we go again," Duncan stated cheerfully, moving to the massive chair.

A group of stylish women in a stunning array of colorful formal dresses and men in tailored tuxedoes spilled out of the elevator car.

Duncan's booming baritone voice rang out. "Ho, ho, ho. Merry Christmas!"

He was really getting into character. Taking her cue, she gestured to the photo booth. "Line up for a picture with Santa. These are a free gift from your host. All photos will be downloadable."

Laughing, several of the guests hurried for the photo op.

She had to give Duncan credit. She could only imagine how much the white facial hair glued to his chiseled jaw prickled. Not to mention the layers of padding beneath the heavy jacket, matching pants and black knee-high boots. He had to be boiling. She was sweating beneath her dress. But he kept the crowd entertained with his jolly quips. The man was charming and competent. She appreciated the latter, but the former annoyed her for some reason.

"Mrs. Claus? Paging Mrs. Claus." Duncan's voice rang loud in her earpiece, cutting through the party's revelry.

Shoulder muscles bunching, Sera stretched her lips back into her fake Mrs. Claus smile and moved to stand in front of the people waiting for their chance to get a picture taken with Santa.

Duncan's chuckle in her ear caused her to raise her eyebrows at him. He grinned, put his finger to his big, bulbous nose and winked.

Barely refraining from rolling her eyes, she said, "Say Rudolph."

The gaggle of women, ranging in age from thirties to seventies, surrounded Santa. "Rudolph!" the women said in unison.

Click, click, click. Sera snapped several pictures. She really hoped not all of these people were criminals. But a jaded part of her was fully aware that most people had something to hide.

As the flow of guests slowed down and the party was going strong, Sera bounced on the balls of her feet to alleviate the ache in her back from standing for the past several hours. Tired and disappointed—so far, Ramon was a no-show—she moved to the table draped in red linen and poured herself a glass of water.

The elevator chimed, indicating another load of late arrivals. Maybe he'd be in this group.

A disturbance behind Sera had her stiffening. Duncan rose from his seat.

"Bogies on your six," Duncan's voice announced in her ear.

Ramon? Anticipation revved her blood.

Sera turned and found herself facing eight, well-armed masked intruders, dressed from head to toe in black. Each had on a backpack—no doubt carrying extra ammo and any other assorted methods of destruction. Steeling herself, she sent up a prayer of protection. This could get ugly.

A collective gasp sounded from the guests. A few screams echoed through the room. The music stopped playing.

The man at the front of the new arrivals spoke in a loud tone, "Merry Christmas, everyone." His voice had a deep, Eastern-European accent. "If everyone cooperates, no one will get hurt."

"I've got the four on the left," Duncan murmured as he stepped to her side.

Assessing the situation and quickly concluding there was no way to take out the bad guys without endangering the civilians, she stopped him with a hand placed on his protruding belly. "Stand down, Santa. Those AK-47s could blow holes in everyone in the room before you could even take two steps."

The last thing she needed was Duncan playing the cowboy.

Duncan itched to reach for the Glock 19 hidden beneath the waistband of his Santa pants. He could fire off four, maybe five, well-placed shots before the goons intruding on the Christmas party could move.

However, Sera was right. The automatic weapons in the masked assailants' hands were formidable obstacles. It was best to make sure everybody stayed calm and they all cooperated. Aware that the rest of the task force could see what was happening, and confident those on the outside were already mobilizing, he stayed put.

"Protect the civilians," he stated, his voice barely above a whisper in acknowledgement of her admonishment that he would've put everyone's lives in jeopardy if he made a move.

"Indeed," she replied dryly. The woman did not like to be told what to do even when he was agreeing with her.

She was a complex woman. A puzzle. A challenge. The deputy marshal was as tough as they came and gave as good as she got. She didn't let him, or anyone else, intimidate her or play her for a fool. All qualities he found rather appealing.

He kept an eye on Sera as she ushered to the middle of the room those who had been frozen in place by their fear.

The undercover officers needed to know what these clearly uninvited people wanted. Taking a chance the intruders wouldn't feel threatened by Santa, Duncan said, "Ho, ho, ho. Merry Christmas to you, too. What can we do for you?"

Sera hissed, "What are you doing?"

"Careful, O'Brien," Gordon Gates murmured into Duncan's ear through the com link. Gordon, a Homeland Security agent and the team leader, was monitoring the operation from the command center in Washington, DC.

Duncan refrained from replying as the man who'd spoken stepped off the elevator platform and moved to stand nose-to-nose with him. The man smelled of fish and desperation.

In his best laid-back-surfer voice, Duncan said, "You're kind of ruining the Christmas vibe here, dude."

He'd perfected the persona on an undercover assignment in Hawaii last year before he'd been brought in on this current task force.

"So Santa's a funnyman," the leader of the group said.

Duncan found the business end of an AK-47 pressed against his padded belly. Tension rippled through him. There wasn't enough padding in the world to stop a round delivered by such a weapon. Duncan held up his white-gloved hands, palms out. Best to acquiesce. "Hey, man, it's all good."

Gesturing with the gun, Gunman Number One said, "Get over there with your missus."

Dismissing Duncan, the man turned to his group and gave a chin nod that sent six of the seven other members of his gang spreading out. They encircled the guests who now clustered in the middle of the lobby floor. The other two undercover members of the task force had taken defensive positions around the perimeter of the civilians while still trying to appear nonthreatening.

Sera jabbed her elbow into his patted rib cage. "You could've gotten yourself killed."

"I didn't know you cared," he murmured, earning himself another jab. "We clearly know who's in charge now. We just need to know what they want."

"Brennan Fleming," Gunman Number One called out. "I'm sure you're here at your own party. Show yourself."

Why would they want Fleming? Did they plan to kidnap him and demand a ransom?

Cindy Kane, the executive assistant who'd hired them, hurried forward, all shimmering and glittery, stilettos echoing on the parquet floor. "I can help you."

"Cindy Kane," the man said in a singsong voice. "Are you as sweet as you look?"

A flash of anger in Cindy's eyes was quickly hidden behind a mask of indifference. "What do you want?"

Gunman Number One strode forward and leaned down right into Cindy's face, grabbing her by the arm.

Duncan's fists curled. He couldn't abide men who abused women.

Sera's hand slipped over one of his fists, covering it in a gentle hold, effectively keeping Duncan from charging forward.

The intruder lowered his voice, but his words still echoed through the room. "I want the pass codes. Every last one of them."

"I don't know what you're talking about," Cindy replied. "What pass codes?"

He shook Cindy. Duncan's blood boiled. Sera stepped on his foot, the momentary pain reeling in his gut-level instinct to protect.

"He's not hurting her," Sera said in a barely audible voice.

But the guy would. And that didn't sit well with Duncan.

"For the offshore accounts," the gunman stated. "Don't play me for a fool." His tone was as sharp as a razor's edge. "I know about them. And I want them."

Cindy's eyes went wide. "I don't have them. Only Brennan has them. And he's not here."

"Why isn't he here?" the man bellowed.

That was a question Duncan wanted an answer to, as well. Brennan Fleming was missing his own holiday party?

"He had a family emergency that has made him late," Cindy said.

"Then you get him here, now," the assailant ordered. "Or I'll start picking off his guests one by one."

A tangible fear rippled over the guests, expressed with quiet sobs and muttered exclamations.

Duncan's gut knotted with apprehension. There was something about this man that made Duncan believe his threat was not empty. Duncan's gaze scanned the other team members. He gave each a subtle nod and received one in turn. No way would they let the man make good on his promise without a fight.

One of the gang members broke rank, walked up to the leader and put a hand on his arm. "Ivan, stick to the plan. Remember the goal. Whoever sows wind reaps storms."

It was a female voice. Curious.

Ivan's mouth twisted. "Smart as always."

Beside Duncan, Sera gasped and her hand over his turned into a vise.

He glanced at her. Beneath her Mrs. Claus costume, her sun-kissed face had drained of color, leaving her ashen.

Gently gripping her bicep with his free hand, he said quietly, "What?"

Her beautiful dark gaze, filled with shock, met his. "That's my sister."

"Your sister?"

Duncan's incredulous question echoed inside Sera's head.

That was Angelina's voice. It had to be. Though this woman's held a deeper timbre brought on by age. Sera also recognized the proverb the woman recited. Their grandmother had often used those exact words as a reminder to think before acting rashly.

"Yes." Disbelief pounded in Sera's chest. "Angelina, my older sister."

How could this be happening? What was her sister mixed up in? Where had she been for two decades?

His eyebrows dipped together. "I didn't know you had a sister. How can you be sure?"

Later, she would decipher the strange note in his voice, but now was not the time to fill him in on the Morales family history. His question gave her pause. Was she sure?

Only one way to find out.

Rapidly strategizing how to separate the woman from the leader—Ivan—Sera broke away from Duncan and stepped forward. Considering she'd possibly ID'd her sister from her voice, Sera altered her own voice slightly. "People have had a lot to drink tonight. Is use of the facilities an option?"

Ivan and the woman both turned to stare at her. Refusing to meet the woman's gaze in case she might recognize her, Sera instead focused on the steely gray eyes of the man in charge as he attempted to stare her into submission.

Not one to back down from anyone, she held his gaze for a long moment.

"Don't challenge him," Duncan's hushed voice ordered through her earpiece.

Heeding the warning despite the way it grated on her nerves, she focused on the weapon in Ivan's hand, recognizing the make and model. An Arsenal SAM7. A reliable, top-notch AK-47 rifle suitable for experienced shooters. At eight and a half pounds and holding a thirty-round banana magazine, the rifle was one of the most expensive legal firearms. Sera doubted Ivan had procured the weapon in a legal fashion.

"Sweetie," the woman said to Ivan, her voice a purr. "Mrs. Claus is right. We should let them use the restrooms."

"Fine," Ivan said, relenting. "You take the women, five at a time."

Giving no sign of recognition, the woman brushed passed Sera to address the huddled guests. "Five of you women to the restrooms. Now."

Sera took a step to follow with the hope of getting the woman alone, but Duncan approached and lightly touched her elbow. "Let the others go first."

He was right, of course. Their top priority was the civilians—keeping them safe and as comfortable as possible in a situation like this.

Ivan took Cindy and another gang member into one of the offices, where Sera supposed the assistant would reach out to her boss, Brennan Fleming.

Waiting for five female guests at a time to use the facilities and return stretched Sera's nerves taut.

"You think this is Los Campeones?" Duncan asked.

"Not their style." Sera had been studying this new drug cartel for months. "They fly under the radar, for the most part. Get in and get out without being seen or leaving any evidence behind."

Which made it difficult to capture any of the members. As far as they could tell, Ramon wasn't one of the men at the party. Had he changed his look? Was he wearing a disguise? Or had he sent one of his lieutenants? One of the men in a fancy tuxedo could be a part of Ramon's inner circle. As far as Sera was concerned, they could be chasing another wild hare into the tall weeds.

However, if this woman turned out to be Angelina, Sera wouldn't begrudge the chase. Not when she might finally be reunited with her sister.

But would the reunion bring more heartache?

More danger?

Most definitely.

She'd have to tread carefully. One misstep could kill them all.

TWO

The last group of women, three in total, headed toward the restroom, prompting Sera to exaggerate the weight of her costume and shuffle forward, with the woman herding them along.

Sera tried to wrap her mind around the idea of her sister as a part of a masked gang of thieves who had intruded on the Fleming Investments Group Christmas party. Why had they chosen this night to show up?

Believing there were no coincidences, Sera couldn't help but speculate maybe Los Campeones was behind this. But as she'd told Duncan, this flashy display wasn't Ramon Vega's style. From her research into the man, he liked to stay on the down-low, rule his territory through swift violence and disappear before anyone could point the finger at him.

Who was this Ivan character?

The facilities were down a long hall lit with motion sensors. Sera hung back, letting the other three glittery, freaked-out females enter the women's restroom ahead of her. Just as the woman took a step for the door, Sera grabbed her arm.

"What are you...?" She shook off Sera's grip.

Before the woman could bring up the muzzle of the AK-47 strapped across her body, Sera had her pinned to the wall with an arm across her throat while her other hand unhooked the strap holding the rifle.

Then Sera released the woman and stepped back, holding the automatic weapon at her side.

The woman rubbed her throat. "Girl, you've got some moves."

"You have no idea," Sera said, letting all the rage, anger and bitterness from twenty years of not knowing where her sister was fill her voice. "Angelina Jolene Morales, what are you doing?"

Behind her mask, dark eyes widened, and she gasped. "How do you know my name? Who are you?"

It *was* Angelina. Outrage and hurt spread through Sera's chest. Why was Angelina a part of this gang? How long had she been in Texas? Sera intended to ask all of these questions.

In Sera's ear, Duncan's voice sounded like a tickle. "Don't push her too hard."

She ignored his warning. She needed answers. A reckoning was long past due. "You really don't recognize me?"

"You're Mrs. Claus," Angelina said dryly. "Hard to see anything but the costume. A bit uninspired, don't you think?"

As tempted as she was to divest herself of her disguise, Sera refrained. Self-preservation had her tempering her emotions and smoothing out her voice. "Are you acting against your will? Are you being threatened?"

Angelina crossed her arms over her chest and glanced

nervously down the hall. "What does it matter to you? How do you know my name?"

Sera refused to believe her sister was willingly involved with these criminals. Angelina had been flighty and rebellious, but not this. There had to be a logical, reasonable explanation as to why Angelina was cooperating with these potentially violent thieves. What compelled her to act so recklessly?

But she didn't know this woman standing before her. Not anymore. Time and distance had changed them both.

"Stay on mission," Gordon Gates ordered. The team leader's voice was soft but firm in her ear.

"Brennan Fleming just arrived," Jackie told them through the com link. "He's in with Ivan and the assistant, Cindy."

Reining in her personal agenda, she asked, "What are you people after? Why are you holding all these guests hostage?"

Angelina studied her. "All it would take is one scream from me and everybody dies. So…" She held out her gloved hand. "Hand it over."

Fearing this might be the last chance she had to discover the truth of what happened to her sister, Sera had to take the opportunity, even knowing she would be tanking her career.

But Angelina was family. A bond that tied them inexplicably together regardless of the differences in their lives.

Sera sent up a quick prayer that God would intervene here. That God would help her find closure for herself and for her parents. She inhaled, bracing herself for what was to come. "Angie, it's me."

Duncan nearly choked in her ear. "Breaking your cover? Really?"

Sera's heart thudded beneath the padded velvet dress. In for a penny, in for a pound. There was no going back. She had this one opportunity and she was taking it. "It's me, Seraphina."

Angelina's hand dropped to her side. Behind her mask, she blinked several times. "Sissy?" She shook her head. "No way."

"Way," Sera said. All the hurt and torment of not knowing what had happened to Angelina roared up, demanding to be heard. "Do you even know the destruction you created in our family when you ran away? How much you hurt us? Did you give any regard to anyone but yourself?"

Angelina put up a hand. "This can't be happening. You're going to get us killed."

With her stomach twisting with grief and fear, and a million other emotions she'd rather not acknowledge, Sera pleaded, "I can get you out of here. I can help you."

"Morales," Gordon hissed. "Enough."

Sera wanted to rip out the ear com and stomp on it.

"You can't help me," Angelina said. "If Ivan finds out I'm talking to you, he'll kill us both. Grace." She shuddered. "Give me the weapon and let me go."

Sera debated telling her sister that she was law enforcement but held back. Instead, she held the automatic weapon by the strap and dangled it from her fingers. "Come get it."

There was just a brief hesitation before Angelina

stepped close. She gripped Sera's hand along with the strap of the weapon. At the same moment, Sera lunged forward, wrapping her free arm around Angelina in a bear hug and dropping the tracker into the side pocket of Angelina's backpack as she whispered in her ear, "I love you."

Angelina jerked back, taking the rifle in her hands. She moved away to push open the restroom door. "Out. Now."

At the other end of the hall, two masked men headed toward them. "What's taking so long?"

Sera held her breath, questioning if her sister would give her up. Preparing to act defensively, she tensed her muscles and took a self-protective stance, thankful the dress masked her body movements.

Angelina waved a hand. "We're all good here, boys." She nudged Sera with the tip of the rifle. "Mrs. Claus had a little wardrobe malfunction."

The two bad guys exchanged a nervous glance.

"You know he'll have our heads if something goes wrong," one of the two men stated, his voice bordering on a whine.

"Petey, you worry too much," Angelina replied. "Come along, ladies."

Sera breathed out a relieved breath as they made their way back to the party.

Duncan's voice filled Sera's head. "You are in so much trouble."

Boy, didn't she know it.

Adrenaline pumped through Duncan's system. He was amped up and ready for a fight. He couldn't believe

Sera had gone rogue, trying to reel in her sister. What was she thinking?

Yet he did sympathize with Sera. Realizing her sibling was involved in criminal activity had to sting. But to break cover? At least Sera hadn't confessed she was in law enforcement. Angelina might very well have ratted her out and exposed the task force.

Didn't Sera understand this was not their circus, not their tigers to cage? The Dallas police would deal with the thieves.

Sera walked back into the lobby with her sister and two other men. Relief was swift but it took all of Duncan's willpower not to rush to her side.

The smart play would be to distance himself from Sera. She could take him down, too.

One word from her sister and they could all be killed. They may have already lost their opportunity to find Ramon Vega.

Yet…he closed his eyes for a moment, sending up a quiet prayer to God asking for wisdom.

It was never the wrong thing to do the right thing.

Sera was his partner. She was the Mrs. Claus to his Santa. And though what might happen once they left this party was uncertain, while they were here in the thick of it, he would have Sera's back.

It was imperative they got out of the situation alive, with no fatalities. Including Sera.

As casually as he could, he strode up to where Sera had paused on the periphery of the gathered guests.

Her gaze was apologetic, but Duncan sensed she would fight for her sister if given half a chance.

Ivan held a small silver thumb drive in his hand as

he walked out of the office and headed to the elevator platform. Apparently, he'd obtained the pass codes and account numbers from Fleming for the many accounts the investment group managed.

Another of Ivan's men had Fleming by the arm and they followed Ivan to the elevator. Fleming, wearing a tuxedo, was in his forties with silver hair. His green eyes were wide and filled with fear. Duncan wanted to feel sorry for the guy, but when you dealt with criminals... Still, he was a civilian and in need of protection. Just how they were going to extract Fleming from Ivan's gang, Duncan wasn't sure.

Angelina joined Ivan at the elevator and whispered in the man's ear.

Duncan's heart thumped. Was Angelina giving up her sister?

The masked man faced the crowd. "Thank you for your cooperation. See, that wasn't so bad. We're not evil. Just trying to make our way in the world. We'll be leaving you now. And we won't see you again." He leveled a finger at Sera. "Mrs. Claus. You're coming with us."

"No!" Duncan wasn't about to let these criminals take Sera.

"It's all right," Sera said, putting her hand on Duncan's forearm. "You'll find me."

Her words slammed into him, reminding him of the tracker in the pocket of her apron over the red, padded dress. One of Ivan's men moved to grasp Sera by the arm and tugged her toward Ivan and Angelina, while a different gunman aimed his rifle at Duncan.

A riot of protective urges surged. "I'm coming, too!"

Ivan laughed. "We don't need Santa. Two hostages are plenty. And if you follow, I'll kill them."

Duncan's heart dropped. No way was he standing idly by while his partner was kidnapped.

As soon as the elevator doors swooshed shut, taking Sera and Fleming, along with her sister and Ivan's gang to the main lobby floor, Duncan said into his ear com, "Please tell me the tracking device is working? Sera is headed to the main lobby."

"It's working but they are going up, not down," said Raphael Fierro, the Italian-born ATF agent who was in a Dallas Police Department surveillance van outside of the building monitoring the camera feeds.

"What?" Duncan ran for the bank of elevators. Sure enough, the elevator Sera had disappeared into was ascending.

"They're going to the roof," Duncan said aloud so their team would know and adjust.

"Roger that," Gordon said. "Letting Dallas PD know."

"In-bound helicopter," Raphael said. "Tail number belongs to City Tours. The bird was reported stolen an hour ago."

There was still a chance Duncan could keep the criminals from leaving. "I'm headed to the roof."

Sera squeezed into the elevator car next to Angelina. Her sister stared at her and shook head, clearly not wanting Sera to speak. The car zoomed upward.

"You don't need me," Brennan Fleming said to Ivan. "You have the account numbers and pass codes on the thumb drive."

One of the masked men rammed the butt of his rifle

into Brennan's gut. Brennan let out a grunt of pain and doubled over.

Sera's hands fisted. There was no way she could subdue seven men in the confined space without someone getting hurt, or worse. Patience wasn't easy for her, but she willed herself to keep a level head. She was confident the task force would monitor her whereabouts, or rather the whereabouts of the tracker that now resided in Angelina's backpack. There would be time to save Brennan and Angelina.

The elevator opened to a service area, where a set of stairs led to the roof access. Ivan and Angelina filed out. Sera and Brennan were pushed forward to follow up the stairs and onto the roof. A chilly wind whipped up by the rotors of an incoming helicopter threatened to lift the wig off Sera's head. She held on to it with one hand.

As the helicopter touched down on the flat expanse of the roof, Ivan turned to his men. "Leave Fleming," he instructed. "Bring Mrs. Claus."

Ivan grabbed Angelina's hand and they ran for the helicopter.

One gunman knocked Brennan unconscious with the side of his weapon. Brennan dropped to the roof like a bag of rocks. Sera winced and prayed the blow wasn't lethal.

Another bad guy wrapped his hand around her right bicep and dragged her to the open door of the helicopter's cabin. She climbed in, squeezing close to Angelina.

Her sister grabbed her hand, and pulled her close and said into Sera's ear, "I'm sorry."

The bird lifted off the ground.

Angelina shoved Sera out the cabin's still open door.

Shock stole Sera's breath. Her arms windmilled as she fell backward into space.

Duncan pushed open the service door to the roof in time to see Sera falling out of the open doorway of the helicopter cabin.

Duncan's heart jumped into his throat. "No!"

At the last second, Sera grabbed the landing rails, dangling for a heart-stopping moment. Thankfully, she let go and crumpled in a heap on the roof. Duncan lunged forward, racing to her side. *Please, God, don't let her be hurt!*

"Sera!" He gathered her to him.

She pushed away, rolling to her feet. "Let me go."

He sat back on his haunches. Clearly, God had heard his plea. The woman appeared uninjured. And feisty as ever.

The building's roof access door banged open, and Dallas PD flooded the roof.

Sera ran for the stairs again.

Now what was she doing?

"Where are you going?" Duncan yelled after her.

"To find my sister!" She disappeared back inside.

His gaze bounced between the open door to the stairs, the retreating helicopter and the officers tending to an unconscious Brennan Fleming.

Dread settled on Duncan's chest like an anvil.

Time to make a choice.

Heart pumping and adrenaline racing through her veins, Sera flew down the service stairs to the bank of elevators. Thankfully, the padding of the costume dress had cushioned her fall from the helicopter enough that she hadn't suffered any serious injuries. No broken bones. Not even a scrape. Undoubtedly, she'd feel the resulting pain from the jarring impact later.

For now, she ignored the aches in her legs and back. Her wig was askew, threatening to fall off completely, but she didn't take time to fix it or pull it off. Why had Angelina pushed her out for the helicopter? To save her? Or to kill her?

Behind Sera, pounding footsteps sounded like a herd of elephants were pursuing her. She didn't need to turn around to know Duncan had followed her. The man wouldn't give up. The elevator doors opened with a *swoosh* and she stepped inside, jamming her finger on the button for the 28th floor.

Before the door closed, Duncan stepped inside. "What's the plan?"

The plan was to track her sister. But she couldn't say that aloud, not with her boss listening in her ear.

The doors slid shut. Duncan leaned back against the wall, folded his arms over his chest and glared at her. She had to give him some sort of answer.

"We use this opportunity to track Ramon Vega," she said.

Duncan arched an eyebrow. "How?"

"Follow the money. One of those accounts has to belong to Vega and Los Campeones." The doors to the elevator opened on the 28th floor. Sera stepped out into the lobby of the Fleming Investments Group. The once crowded and festive space was nearly empty. Nothing like armed invaders to end a party. Only the task force members and Fleming's assistant, Cindy Kane, remained.

Not waiting for Duncan, Sera marched to where Cindy, dressed in a glittery green dress that made her look like a Christmas lightbulb, was talking with Jackie and another task force member, FBI Agent Trevor Winfield. He was a lanky, well-built former college athlete dressed in a waiter's uniform of black slacks and a white dress shirt with a black bow tie.

"Your boss will be taken to the hospital," Sera said to Fleming's assistant.

Cindy's mouth gaped and tears welled in her eyes. "He's okay?"

"He took a blow to the head, but I saw a policeman checking his pulse and indicating he was alive," Sera said.

Cindy reached for a nearby table to steady herself. "That's good. I was so worried. I have to tell his wife and family. His daughter just had a baby tonight, that's why he was late."

"You need to give us everything you gave to Ivan and his men," Sera said.

"Only Brennan has access to the accounts they wanted," she said.

Sera gritted her teeth. They needed to know where those funds were coming from and where they were being transferred to. She could probably hack into the system, but it would take time. Time she didn't have. Not if she wanted to find her sister before it was too late.

"Raphael." Sera turned to Duncan. "He could hack the system." Raphael was better with technology, which she wasn't too proud to admit.

"I'd have to come up there," Raphael said into the com link embedded in Sera's ear.

That's exactly what Sera was counting on. "I'll trade places with you."

Without waiting for confirmation, Sera rushed to grab her duffel bag, which was stowed beneath the photo staging area table. Beside her, Duncan grabbed his bag.

She held up a hand when he moved to follow her to the elevator. "You should stay here and oversee everything."

"You're not getting rid of me that easily," he stated. "We're partners. Remember?"

Inwardly, she groaned. He was never going to let her do what she needed to do. She had to ditch him. But how? She could tell him the truth. But not with her boss in her ear. "I need to get out of this ridiculous costume. I'll change in the van."

The stall tactic would at least keep him at bay long enough for her to grab the GPS unit now tracking her sister.

Duncan pressed the down button for the elevator. "Whatever floats your boat."

Outside on the street, in front of the large office building, chaos reigned. The party guests were giving statements to various police officers while a few gawkers stopped their Christmas shopping to see what was happening. Sera ducked beneath the crime-scene tape and hustled across the street to the unmarked utility van parked at the curb. She wrapped her knuckles on the back door and it swung open to reveal Raphael.

The tall, dark, handsome man, dressed in his signature black turtleneck and black jeans, grinned at her.

"Seeing you two together gives the Santa and Mrs. Claus gig a whole other dimension. Sweet."

She waved away his comment like she would a gnat. "Get up there. We need to track that money before it's gone. Ivan said he wanted all the pass codes to all the accounts. One of those accounts has to belong to Los Campeones."

From behind her, Duncan said, "We don't even know *if* any of the cartels are really running money through the Fleming Investments Group."

Holding on to her patience by a thin thread, she turned to face him. "And we don't know they aren't. It was your informant who told us about the Fleming Investments Group and the connection to Ramon. Do you believe he lied?"

Duncan made a face. "Confidential informants lie all the time. But this one—my gut tells me no. He wasn't lying."

"I'll leave you two to hash this out while I find out what I can about the money trail," Raphael said then hopped out of the van and jogged across the street.

Sera grasped the back door handle and hiked her leg to step on the back bumper. Aches that she'd been ignoring from falling out of the helicopter protested the movement. A small gasp of pain escaped.

Strong hands circled her waist and lifted her into the van.

She jerked away. "I don't need your assistance."

Duncan lifted his hands, palms out. "Sorry. Figured it was most expedient to just lift you. I won't do that again."

Guilt pricked her. He was only trying to help. She didn't need to keep biting his head off. But he was getting in her way and it made her cranky. She grabbed the door handle. "I'm going to change out of this costume. You stay out here."

She slammed the door shut in his face and took a breath, held it a moment, then slowly let it out in an effort to calm her racing heart. Adrenaline still pumped through her veins, but she was grateful because when it wore off, she had a feeling her body was going to let her know exactly what landing on the roof had done to her.

Enclosed within the surveillance van, she removed the glasses with the hidden camera and set them face down on the ledge next to the video monitors. Then she quickly searched for the handheld GPS unit that would allow her to track the small disc she had planted on her sister. She found the palm-size device and was thankful Raphael hadn't noticed the dot was zooming away from downtown Dallas. But where was Angelina headed? Would Sera be able to track her down? Would Ivan release her sister without a fight?

A shudder of dread ran down Sera's spine. She took a deep breath to calm herself. She needed to get a grip because her first order of business was to ditch Duncan.

THREE

Sera listened for any sound of Duncan outside of the van. She could imagine him impatiently waiting for her to change. He was going to have to wait a little longer. She stared at the GPS unit and watched the dot traveling in the same direction, taking her sister farther away. Sera contemplated her next move.

She needed wheels and the van was right here. But the minute she fired up the engine, her boss, along with everyone else on the team, would know what she was doing. She plucked the communication device from her ear and buried it inside a discarded chip bag she found in the garbage can.

There was a banging at the back door. Duncan. After stashing the tracking unit in her duffel bag, she opened the door.

"Why haven't you changed?" He'd removed his Santa hat and unbuttoned the red jacket to reveal the large pillow strapped to his torso.

She grimaced. "I got distracted. I'll change later. You go ahead."

Ignoring his outstretched hand, she jumped out, landing easily beside him. A ripple of uncomfortable tension zinged through her muscles. She gritted her teeth against the sensation.

He shook his head and climbed into the van, shutting the door softly. She stood there for a moment, clutching her duffel to her chest. She needed to get away from here.

With slow measured steps, she backed up until she was in the shadow of the building behind her. Then she quickly hurried down the sidewalk, the dress flapping against her legs as she rounded the corner.

Her way was lit by the festive lights adorning the trees and lamp posts lining the sidewalk. Large wreaths hung from the streetlight poles.

She dug out her smartphone to pull up the Yellow Cab DFW app, and hit the drop icon for her location. Within seconds, the app had a cab headed in her direction.

As she tapped her foot, anxiety twisted in her gut. She had to get into the cab and away before Duncan realized she was gone. The man was relentless. For the months they'd been working together, she'd observed him pursue each lead with dogged determination.

Once he set his mind to something, he didn't stop until he accomplished his goal, or refocused on a new task. Admirable traits. She just didn't like being the one he was focused on. He would only get in her way.

A bright yellow minivan pulled to the curb. She slid inside the back passenger seat.

"Where to, miss? Or should I say Mrs. Claus?" the taxi driver asked with a smile.

"One second." She unzipped the duffel and brought out the GPS unit. She pushed a button and the device beeped to life, the annoying sound grating on her nerves. The stationary dot revealed her sister was no longer traveling. She'd apparently reached her destination. Sera zoomed in on the screen to see the cross streets.

She gave the taxi driver the address while keeping her gaze glued to the little red dot.

The taxi began to move and then stopped abruptly.

Sera looked up to find Duncan blocking the vehicle, a fierce expression on his ruggedly handsome face. She was so busted.

She cringed. Duncan had removed his beard and white wig to reveal his strong jaw and dark brown hair, which was slicked back and mashed to his head. The padded pillow was no longer strapped to his torso. He had on a black, long-sleeve T-shirt, along with the red Santa pants and black knee-high boots. Even in such a ridiculous outfit, he looked good. Why did she find him so attractive? She gritted her teeth with frustration. How had he known where she was?

Duncan circled the taxi and opened the sliding back door. He folded his big frame onto the bucket seat next to her.

"Where are we going?" His voice was deceptively soft and calm, but Sera could feel the waves of tension radiating off him like nuclear waste.

Not about to say a word for fear he still had his earpiece in, she grabbed his face, turning his head from side to side as she looked in his left ear, then his right. No com link. She breathed a sigh of relief.

He grasped her hands, removing them from his face. "Sera?"

Tugging her hands free, she sat back and folded her arms over her chest. "How did you know?"

He snorted and copied her posture. "How could I not?"

She rolled her eyes. He was always so quick with the comebacks.

The taxi driver turned around to stare at them. He was an older gentleman with kind eyes. "Do you still need a ride?"

Duncan arched an eyebrow at her. She was beginning to dislike that arched eyebrow that seemed to mock her. She held up a finger to the driver, indicating for him to wait a moment longer. To Duncan, she said, "You need to get out. This doesn't concern you."

"Where you go, I go," he told her.

"I can't be responsible for you," she snapped. She was willing to tank her career and put her life at risk, but not his.

"But *I* am responsible for *you*."

Her gut churched with acid. "I'm off the clock now."

Duncan's mouth twisted, drawing her gaze. He really was a handsome man. "The boss feels that way. He made that very clear."

Jerking her gaze to meet his, she seethed with outrage. "You told Gordon?"

Holding up his hands, palms out, he replied, "More like he told me."

Her heart sank. How could that be? "What?"

Duncan shrugged. "The video camera outside the building showed you hurrying away from the van."

She gnashed her teeth. She should've thought of the video feeds surrounding the building, but she'd been so intent on getting away and getting to her sister, she hadn't fully considered all the variables. That was not like her. She usually was more strategic and detail oriented. This situation was messing with her head. And her judgment.

"Really, Duncan." She infused her voice with deep sincerity. "You have a whole career ahead of you. A good career. Don't mess it up on my account. I'm not worth it."

"Too late," he said. He turned to the driver. "Go wherever it is she told you to go. Step on it."

The taxi shot forward.

"You might as well come clean with me."

His gentle voice abraded her nerves. Why was he doing this? Did he have no sense of self-preservation? The man should be running in the other direction.

She debated telling him everything. If it was Jace Armstrong or Brian Forrester, she wouldn't think twice about divulging the details. Her fellow marshals were her best friends. Her surrogate family.

But her sister was also her family, even if Angelina had turned her back and walked away from Sera years ago.

Sera would not rest until she had closure. One way or another, she had to talk to Angelina again.

Did she dare trust Duncan? Would he try to stop her?

"I'd like to know what we're getting ourselves into," he continued, his tone adamant. "To be prepared."

He did deserve to know what they would be walking into. He was not going to like it. She couldn't worry about that. He'd made the decision to tag along. But she didn't want him to get hurt, either.

"I know where Angelina is," she told him, bracing herself for his reaction.

His jaw firmed and his eyes narrowed. "And how exactly do you know this?"

Grimacing, she pulled out the small handheld device from her duffel bag and held it up. "This."

Realization widened his eyes. He shook his head. "You dropped the tracker meant for Ramon Vega onto your sister somehow."

Not surprised he'd worked it out so quickly, she lifted her chin and owned up to what she had done. "I did. I put it in her backpack."

He slapped a hand to his forehead in exasperation. "Are you always this rash? Using government equipment for your personal agenda will not win you any favors."

Heat burned her cheeks. "I know that. I'm not looking for favors or approval. My agenda is to find my sister."

She turned and faced him. The short distance between them, within the confines of the back of the cab, was too intimate, almost too uncomfortable for her to bear. But bear it, she would. He'd made it clear he wasn't abandoning her to her own devices. He was sticking close. So she needed him to be on board with this and not hinder her.

"Consider the situation this way," she said, hoping to appeal to his sense of logic. "We get Angelina, we get Ivan. We get the accounts. Which will ultimately lead us to Ramon and Los Campeones."

Duncan threw up his hands, his disbelief apparent. "That's a lot of speculation and conjecture. You better hope this thread pulls through and it's easy to tie off."

"I'm praying with everything in me that we can bring

down Los Campeones." And she was also praying for a
chance to extract her sister from the clutches of Ivan.

Angelina had been scared of the man. Hearing her
asking God for grace had warmed Sera's heart. Her
sister still had faith. She had to be acting under duress.
Angelina wasn't a criminal. Sera refused to believe it,
but she couldn't help but consider the possibility she
was deluding herself.

Feeling conspicuous in the ridiculous bright red pants
and knee-high boots, tension coiled inside Duncan like
a rattler about to strike. Staying alert to their surroundings, he stepped out of the back of the taxi and surveyed
the warehouse behind a chain-link fence. They were in
a warehouse district outside the city limits. At this time
of night, the area was quiet and deserted.

A light fixture near the building's door glowed bright.
The glow reflected off the windows lining the wall of the
structure. The outline of a helicopter on the roof against
the backdrop of the night sky confirmed that the red dot
had led them to the place Ivan and his people had escaped to. The taxi took off, as if the driver couldn't get
out of there fast enough.

Sera stepped closer to the fence. She barely reached
the top of Duncan's shoulders, but she was a power-
house and easy to underestimate. Her scheme of getting
to her sister and Ivan, and hoping that would eventually
lead to bringing down Los Campeones, skirted sound
reasoning. But she was so convinced and determined, he
doubted anything or anyone would be able to stop her.

"What are we expecting to accomplish here?" He
hoped she had a plan. Something other than just barg-

ing in and demanding the information to those bank accounts. Or, worse yet, insisting her sister leave with her. He had a feeling neither one of those two things was going to happen without repercussions that might get them killed.

"Recon," she said. "We call for backup if things get hairy."

"It's going to get hairy." Tingles started at the back of his neck and ran down his spine. A clear indication that his instincts were on high alert.

He didn't like this situation at all. But someone had to keep her from getting captured or killed. He could see why she was a good US Marshal. She was fearless, determined and willing to take risks to get the job done.

He was all for getting the job done, but he wasn't as eager to take such huge risks. He planned to see old age. Hopefully with a family, but that was far into the future. He couldn't let himself dwell on the fact that he wasn't in a relationship. He hadn't met anyone in a long time that he wanted to pursue.

Ignoring him, Sera circled the fence surrounding the building, clearly looking for an entry point. The place was locked up tight. The only way in was through the locked gate.

Planting her hands on her hips, she glanced over her shoulder at him. "Can you give me a boost?"

Of course, she'd want to go over the obstacle in her path. "It could be electrified."

She searched the ground until she found a rock and heaved it at the fence. The rock bounced off the chain link without sparks. "Let me stand on your shoulders, then I'll slip over and see what's inside the warehouse."

He barked out a quiet laugh, though there was no humor behind it. "Right. Like we're acrobatic street performers? I don't think so."

"Come on," Sera cajoled. "You're afraid, aren't you? I'm not. You won't drop me. And the jump on the other side is minimal. I survived a fall from a helicopter—this will be a cakewalk."

No, he wouldn't drop her, but she might crush him under the weight of her recklessness. And, of course, she'd consider the drop minimal. She probably leaped tall buildings in her spare time just for fun.

Screeching tires on pavement echoed through the stillness of the night. Duncan grabbed Sera and they hunched down behind a stack of discarded oil drums just as a bevy of muscle cars and tricked-out SUVs parked in front of the fence.

"Who are these guys?" Sera whispered.

Before Duncan could answer, men with automatic rifles exited the vehicles and shot up the front of the warehouse. The deafening noise assaulted Duncan's ears and he instinctively tucked himself around Sera to shield her.

Answering shots volleyed back from the broken warehouse's windows. Bullets were coming from both directions and hitting way too close for comfort. They were in a precarious position, where one stray round could be the end of either of them.

What had they stumbled into? Was this a turf war?

A moment of silence filled the air as both sides stopped shooting. Duncan's ears rang, a sensation he didn't enjoy.

Ivan's voice called out from within the warehouse. "Tell Vega I didn't know. I won't touch any of his money."

"My boss wants everything you took from Fleming." There was no mistaking the heavy Spanish accent of the man shouting back.

In answer, another barrage of gunfire erupted from the warehouse.

"Now would be a good time to call for help," Duncan muttered.

Sera elbowed him, forcing him to give her room. She whipped out a cell phone from the pocket of her padded costume dress and dialed. "Raphael, we need backup. Pronto. Sending you the address now."

Duncan wasn't holding his breath that the team would make it to the scene in time to aid him and Sera. They were going to have to get out of the situation on their own.

He had to get Sera out of there or they were going to be mincemeat. He didn't like the Christmas pie and certainly didn't want to be responsible for Sera's death. Seeing a dumpster in the next lot, he decided they needed to make a run for it.

Hefting Sera's duffel bag over his shoulder and latching on to her, he urged her to run deep into the inky darkness away from the gunfire.

"Hey!" a voice yelled.

More gunfire erupted, this time directed at them.

Staying low, Duncan pulled Sera behind the dumpster. His eyes watered at the rancid odor wafting from the refuse receptacle. "I'd say we found Los Campeones."

"You think?" Her dry tone scraped along his nerves.

Another sound permeated the air. The sound of rotors coming to life. The helicopter Ivan and Angelina had escaped in before lifted off the roof of the ware-house and once again disappeared into the night sky.

"No!" The word burst from Sera.

Tightening his hold on her, he said, "No more going rogue."

"But—"

"No. Your stubborn willfulness will come back to bite you one day."

"Maybe," she snapped. "But today is not that day."

Growling softly, he said, "Now we play by the rules. Ivan and Los Campeones are at odds with each other. Your theory of Ivan stealing Ramon's money is spot on. You may wiggle out of this fiasco intact, after all."

The sound of approaching footsteps shuddered through him. He grabbed for the Glock at the back of his waistband. "But first we have to survive the night."

Sera tensed, every muscle in her body rigid. Ignoring the stench wrapping around her, she pressed her back against the cold metal of the dumpster and breathed through her mouth. Lifting her gaze to the sky, she searched for the helicopter, but it had long disappeared. Was her sister on it? Or had she managed to escape on foot? Could she still be inside the building, possibly hurt? Or worse?

Heavy footfalls sounded like the toll of the grim reaper, coming closer to Sera and Duncan's hiding spot.

Sera closed her eyes and concentrated on the noise. Sounded like the guy was alone. She and Duncan needed to capture him to get intel on Los Campeones. As much as it galled her to admit, Duncan may be right. She might be able to salvage her career, after all.

She tapped Duncan on the shoulder and his attention swiveled toward her. She gestured for him to go left, and she'd go right. She leaned in close and whispered, "Capture him."

Duncan grasped her hand and pulled her closer. "No."

Sera frowned, tugging her hand to break free of his hold. No? Why? Snagging the guy was a good plan.

With her duffel bag slung over one shoulder, Duncan nudged Sera to move in a crouch around to the end of the dumpster. She gritted her teeth with frustration. Taking down fugitives was in her wheelhouse. Together, she and Duncan could quickly and quietly subdue their quarry and spirit him away from the area for interrogation.

The foot soldier rounded the dumpster, and was now standing in the exact spot where Sera and Duncan had been. With her heart hammering like a hummingbird on steroids, Sera prepared to pounce. Duncan gripped her biceps just as another man joined the first one.

Surprise and disconcertment flooded Sera. She rocked back on her heels. She hadn't heard the second guy's approach. But somehow, Duncan had. A mix of annoyance and admiration threaded through her veins. She was off her game. She'd better get it together or she would get them killed.

"I know I saw someone over here," one of the men said in rapid Spanish.

"The boss wants us to fan out," the other man replied in English. "If any of those thieving rats got away, we'll catch them. Nobody takes our money and lives to spend it."

Sera itched to grab the man by the scruff and demand

answers. How had Los Campeones known about Ivan and his gang so quickly? How had they found them? Where was Ramon Vega? And, more importantly, where was Angelina?

Sirens filled the air as Dallas police cruisers approached the scene. The two men took off at a run, back toward their vehicles.

Sera itched to follow but Duncan's hand tightened around her arm, keeping her in place. The world went quiet as the sound of the wailing sirens ended. Blowing out her frustration in a noisy exhale, Sera rose. How were they going to explain this to the local police?

Headlights coming toward them made her shield her eyes. No flashing lights of a police cruiser. Was this friend or foe?

Duncan stood and pushed her behind him. She batted at his shoulders. She didn't need him protecting her like some damsel in distress.

An SUV roared down the street and stopped beside them.

The front passenger window slid down. Raphael leaned from the driver's side and said, "Get in."

Sera pushed past Duncan and hurried to the vehicle, hopping into the front seat. Duncan climbed into the back passenger seat with her duffel bag in tow. The SUV rolled away from the warehouse in the opposite direction of Los Campeones.

"Shouldn't we follow the cartel?" she asked.

"Not the directive the boss gave us," Raphael stated and stepped on the gas.

"Were you able to duplicate what Brennan Fleming gave to Ivan?" Sera asked.

"No, unfortunately," Raphael said. "The hard drives have been wiped clean. The assistant said the network backup has been corrupted. The flash drive is the only evidence linking Los Campeones, or anyone else, for that matter, to Fleming."

Sera smacked her hand against the dashboard. "This is a colossal mess."

"We're alive." Duncan leaned forward and put a hand on her shoulder. "For now, that has to be enough. And we know that Ivan and his team stole from Los Campeones. You were right—we have to follow the money. We do that by bringing in Ivan."

Yes, she was right. Little comfort. She cared more about finding her sister. But she wouldn't put voice to that thought. She didn't want to slip any lower in Duncan's estimation.

"We could've captured the guy," Sera groused and shrugged off his hand. "He could have led us right to Vega."

"Hello! Exactly how would we have managed to get out of there dragging a suspect with us?" Duncan asked. "He would've been missed. As it was, one of his 'friends' joined him. The moment the second guy realized his buddy wasn't there, we'd have had the whole of Los Campeones on our tail."

She hated to admit he was right. "Still, we could have extracted intel from one or both of them about Ramon and Ivan." Which ultimately would lead her to Angelina.

"And doubled our chances of getting caught," Duncan replied. "I've been doing my job long enough to know when to dip out in order to stay alive."

Was he suggesting she hadn't been on the job long enough to know when to cut bait? She was an experienced marshal. She had commendations and had been picked for this task force because she was good at her job. "You don't believe we could have handled those two?"

"Of course, we could have handled those two, but not the rest of the cartel swarming around like hornets," Duncan said. "I didn't want to kick the nest."

Sera rolled her eyes. He played too cautiously. If she'd have been with her fellow deputy marshals, they'd have extracted both men and mined them for information.

"Enough." Raphael's voice held a good dose of amusement. "It's hard to believe you two have only known each other for less than a year. You bicker like an old married couple."

There was nothing funny about the situation. It hadn't taken her more than a few days to realize she and Duncan weren't compatible. They approached the job, and life, from different angles. Grating against each other was inevitable. Fuming, she turned her thoughts back to her sister. Why was Angelina with Ivan? How had she ended up in this mess?

The handheld GPS unit was tucked away in the duffel bag. "Please give me the bag."

"You looking for this?" Duncan held up the tracking device.

She snatched the unit from his hands and watched the blinking dot move rapidly across the screen. Angelina was indeed still in the helicopter.

Would they leave the city? Depending on the cellular coverage of where the helicopter landed, the GPS tracker could lose the signal and then Sera would lose her sister. Again.

And she'd have thrown away her career for nothing and earned herself more misery.

FOUR

The ride back to the house where the special task force had set up their command post on the outskirts of Dallas was fraught with a tense silence so thick it seemed even the air was heavy. Duncan breathed through his frustration. The night had been a major hot mess. First, Duncan's confidential informant's information hadn't panned out. No Ramon Vega, no Los Campeones.

Then masked thieves had crashed the party. As if that alone wasn't bad enough, Sera's sister ended up being one of the thieves and Sera had put her career at risk hoping to bring in her sister from the cold. Against his better judgment, Duncan had gone along with Sera, fearing for her safety.

And what did they have to show for their efforts?

Sera sat rigid in the front seat, her gaze focused straight ahead, and her hands fisted around the blinking GPS unit in her lap. There was no reasoning with the bold and brash woman. He couldn't wrap his mind around her need to apprehend and interrogate cartel members on the fly without a plan or backup. That was how operatives died.

Soon, Duncan and Sera were going to have to face their boss, Gordon Gates. He would not be happy when he discovered Sera had been tracking her sister. But hopefully, learning of Los Campeones's interest in Ivan and his gang would mollify Gordon. Duncan only hoped he and Sera could salvage their careers from this debacle.

A buzzing in his ears attested to the rise in his blood pressure. He shook his head, pulled on his earlobes and worked to calm his breathing. The noise persisted, penetrating past the cacophony of gunfire that had made his hearing a bit fuzzy.

He rolled down the window. The sound grew louder. Familiar. Like one of the surveillance drones he'd used in various operations in the past.

"Do you hear that sound?" he asked the others.

"These tires are run flats," Raphael stated. "They hum."

"No, that's not what I'm hearing. Can you stop?"

The SUV slowed to a halt on the soft dirt shoulder of the country road leading to the task force house.

"What's going on?" Sera asked as she removed the wig and bonnet, revealing her dark hair rolled into a smashed bun on top of her head.

Duncan held up a hand to silence her as he popped open the door and stepped out. He cocked his head and listened. The noise receded, fading into nothingness. The sky was clear, the air smelled rich with earthy scents he'd come to associate with Texas. There were no other vehicles on the road. Had there been a drone? Or was he being paranoid?

"Duncan?" Sera joined him.

Running a hand over his jaw, the bristles of his day's beard scraping his palm, he said, "I thought… I guess it was nothing."

She touched his arm. "We should go."

Great, now she probably worried about his competency.

They arrived at the large ranch-style home on three acres that had been leased for the task force. Raphael pulled the SUV into the garage.

Duncan climbed out, ready for a hot shower and a change of clothes. Sera shut the SUV passenger door then jammed the GPS unit into the pocket of her apron. Duncan raised an eyebrow at her.

"What?" She gave him a look that matched the defensiveness clear in her tone.

Shaking his head at her stubborn refusal to see reason, he said, "You know what."

"I'll turn it in," she muttered. "Just as soon as I have a bead on where my sister lands."

Stubborn and relentless. Duncan respected her tenacity but feared it would get her fired. Or worse, killed. And him along with her.

She headed inside, leaving him to follow in her wake.

A bank of computer monitors dominated the living room, dwarfing the brown leather couch and armchairs that faced a gas fireplace where someone had hung red-and-white stockings. A festive Christmas tree in front of the window had been decorated with lights, popcorn strung on fishing wire and generic-colored balls. The gleaming lights from the Christmas tree provided by the rental company reminded him this was supposed to be the most wonderful time of year.

If only he could relax and enjoy the specialness of the season and the true reason for celebrating—the birth of Jesus. But that would have to wait. He sent up a prayer this mission would be over by Christmas Day. Not that he had anyone special to spend the holiday with. His parents were off on their traditional Christmas cruise, and he had no siblings.

Usually, in whatever city he happened to be in at the time, he would volunteer at a church that provided meals for those without homes. If he was still here in Dallas on Christmas Day, he would find somewhere to be of service. He tore his gaze away from the tree and moved into the dining room.

Financial reports were spread across the large dining table. Christmas music played softly in the background. The house had five bedrooms to accommodate the five task force members in residence. Their boss was located in Washington, DC. The space was more comfortable than most of the undercover accommodations he'd used previously in his career.

Sera headed toward for the hallway that would lead to her room.

"Morales." the deep voice of FBI Agent Trevor Winfield halted her steps. "The boss wants a word."

Duncan itched to change out of the velvet Santa pants and black knee-high boots, but it would have to wait. He'd promised Sera he'd have her back.

Sera swiveled, lifted her chin and moved to the dining area.

Their boss's face filled the 52-inch monitor on the wall. He was in his late fifties, with graying hair, steely eyes that could cut glass and a scar slashed across his chin. The rumor was he'd been injured during an operation protecting a sitting president. But no one could confirm for sure…and no one was going to ask. Gordon Gates wasn't the type of man to invite idle chitchat or personal inquiries.

"Sit rep," Gordon said.

"Sir, if I may," Duncan began, hoping to reframe the situation report in a way that didn't leave him and Sera without jobs.

"No," Gordon barked out. "Deputy Morales. Speak."

Sera's jaw tightened and she let out a breath. Flipping back the long strands of hair that had slipped from her messy bun, she stepped forward. "Sir, I can explain."

Gordon arched a dark brown eyebrow. "Then do."

Duncan moved to stand beside her, offering her his silent support. She slowly turned her head to stare at him with a question in her dark eyes, then refocused on the man leading their task force.

"As you heard, my sister, Angelina, is somehow involved with this gang of thieves who crashed the Fleming Investments Group's Christmas party and stole from the firm's clients," Sera said in a modulated manner that suggested she was trying hard to keep her emotions from entering her voice.

Duncan's heart twisted. He wished he could make this better for her. Though why he should feel the need was a mystery. It wasn't like they had anything in common, and they barely could tolerate being in the same space together. But he couldn't deny there was something special about Seraphina Morales that intrigued him. He couldn't remember the last time he'd been so drawn to a woman.

"Yes, we are all aware of your sister's involvement," Gordon intoned with a good dose of censure that, even through a video screen, held a punch. "We have run a background check on her. But there is nothing after her sixteenth birthday."

Pain marched across Sera's face and Duncan fought the urge to wrap an arm around her. She'd probably punch him if he tried, so he locked his hands behind his back and rocked on the heels of his boots. How had Angelina remained off the grid for so many years?

"Yes, sir. She ran away when she was sixteen. I have not seen her since. Until tonight."

"Why did you sneak away from the van?" Gordon's eyes narrowed.

Sera slanted a glance at Duncan, revealing a moment of panic, but then the look hardened into determination. He gave her an encouraging nod, hoping she would come clean, and hoping to let her know he was on her side.

"While I had Angelina alone," she said, "I put the tracker meant for Ramon Vega into my sister's backpack. I was following it."

"As it turns out, sir," Duncan interjected, "one of the accounts attached to the stolen pass codes belongs to Los Campeones. Just as Deputy Morales had theorized."

Gordon's chin dipped. "I don't recall hearing that theory until after the fact."

"I wasn't sure." She slanted Duncan an annoyed glance.

He pressed his lips together to keep from grinning. She may not want his help, but she was getting it, anyway.

She continued, "I take full responsibility for my actions. I acted emotionally. It was unprofessional of me."

"Yes, you did. And, yes, it was. I'd like you to pack your bags. You're headed back to San Antonio. Marshal Gavin Armstrong can deal with you. I can't have someone unreliable on the team." Gordon leaned back as if the conversation was over and crossed his arms.

Duncan's heart thudded in his chest. He stepped forward so that his shoulder bumped against Sera's. He fully expected her to retreat, but she stayed in place. "Sir, it would be a mistake to dismiss Deputy Morales."

Gordon snapped to attention, his face taking up the whole screen as he leaned forward. "Excuse me?"

Focusing on the man who held his and Sera's fate in his hands, Duncan threaded steel through his own voice. There was too much at stake to let the investigation into Los Campeones be derailed now. Duncan had his own reasons for wanting to stop the flow of drugs.

"Deputy Morales's actions have garnered us a lead. One we didn't have before. We can follow that tracking device and it will lead us to the flash drive with the accounts. We need to locate and capture Ivan before Los Campeones does. Squeeze him for intel. Then we leverage the accounts to bring in Ramon Vega."

Duncan ignored the daggers Sera stared at him.

Gordon's harsh gaze seemed to reach through the video feed to pin Duncan to the spot. When Gordon didn't say anything right away, Duncan continued, "Los Campeones won't rest until they punish those who dared steal from them. Following Sera's sister is our best course of action. Does it matter how we got here if the circumstances further our ultimate goal of dismantling Los Campeones and bringing down Ramon Vega?"

Gordon grunted. "You make a compelling argument, Agent O'Brien."

"Sir, I—" Sera began, but Gordon held up his hand, staying her words.

"I will allow Deputy Morales to stay on the task force." He lifted a finger and pointed it at Sera. "But you will be kept on a very short leash."

Sera had the good sense to incline her head in acknowledgment of the reprieve. "Yes, sir."

"O'Brien, you stick to her like a tick. Don't let her shake you off. She is not to leave your sight. You find the sister, you find Ramon Vega."

Gordon clicked off and the big-screen TV went dark.

Blowing out a relieved breath, Duncan said, "That went better than I expected."

Sera's gaze turned to him. Thunderclouds gathered in her dark eyes. "I don't need you going to bat for me."

He crossed his arms over his chest. "Clearly, you *do* need me. Despite not wanting me. We are a team. You're my partner. End of story. Because without me, you'd be heading to San Antonio."

And for some reason, the thought of Sera being kicked off the task force and out of his life left Duncan with a bitter taste in his mouth.

Contrition zinged through Sera. Duncan was right *again*. So irritating. If he hadn't spoken up and argued with their boss, she'd be packing her bags. Through gritted teeth, she managed to respond to him. "Thank you. I'm going to get out of this costume. Then, will you please help me locate my sister?"

The tender light in his blue eyes rubbed at the edges of her agitation. "Of course. I'm in with both feet. I'll meet you back here in twenty minutes."

He walked away, heading to his room behind the kitchen. She sighed. What was it about this man that flummoxed her so badly?

From the moment they'd met, when the special unit had been formed, there'd been this undercurrent of competition, of one-upmanship, that stretched her nerves taut. The former economics major turned DEA agent never relented. And he was too good-looking to be trusted. Not that she'd trust him even if he wasn't good-looking.

Trust was a commodity she possessed little of and she only dispensed it when that trust was earned. She still hadn't decided what to make of Duncan. But he'd had her back tonight. She wouldn't forget it.

In her room at the end of the hall at the opposite end of the house, she quickly disrobed, leaving the costume in an untidy lump on the floor. After showering and braiding her damp hair, she dressed in black cargo pants and a lightweight black sweater, which she retrieved from her go bag. December nights could be cold in Dallas. She stuffed zip ties in one of her pants pockets. She attached her holster with her Glock to her waist and grabbed her jacket.

Seeing the mess she'd made of the costume, she grimaced and hung up the padded red dress. Then she picked up the once-white apron that now was smudged with grime and dirt. She folded the apron, and something fell to the floor at her feet.

Bending to pick it up, her breath lodged in her chest. A silver flash drive.

Had Angelina put it in Sera's pocket before pushing her from the helicopter? She must have. Last time Sera had seen the device, it had been in Ivan's hand. Had Angelina somehow taken it from Ivan?

Which meant that Angelina was in danger.

A buzzing noise filled Sera's head. Before she could decide what to do, the lights in the house winked out.

Duncan's heart pounded in his chest. The house was dark. Had the electricity been cut? The annoying noise of a surveillance drone hovering outside the task force house sent chills of dread sliding down his spine. He hadn't been mistaken and the lack of electricity wasn't a fluke. He had heard a drone and they'd been followed. The question was, by whom? Los Campeones? Or Ivan's gang?

With his hands out in front of him to keep from running into anything, Duncan made his way out of his room and through the kitchen. His eyes quickly adjusted to the ambient light streaming through the edges of the curtains.

Trevor jammed a set of night-vision goggles into his hand. "Here."

Grateful, Duncan slipped them on over his eyes and the world lit up in a luminous green. In the living room, now he could see Jackie crouched beside the Christmas tree looking out the front window while Raphael took a position near the door and peered out the sidelight. Each of them had on NVGs and held weapons at the ready.

"I see movement," Jackie stated. "At least ten armed men."

Duncan scanned the room. His heart revved. "Where's Sera?"

"Down the hall," Trevor replied.

Duncan raced down the hallway just as Sera emerged from her room. They collided. He gripped her by the shoulders. She'd braided her hair and changed into dark clothes. The fresh scent of her shampoo teased his senses. "Are you okay?"

"Of course." She gripped his forearms. "What's happening?"

"We *were* followed." He took her by the hand and they joined their teammates. "I was sure I heard a drone on our way in."

Trevor handed Sera NVGs and she pulled the goggles over her head and adjusted them to cover her eyes.

A disembodied voice rang out in the quiet darkness. "Send out Mrs. Claus with the flash drive or we'll burn you down."

"What are they talking about?" Duncan demanded.

Sera held up a silver thumb drive. "My sister must have dropped the flash drive into the pocket of my apron when I was on the helicopter."

"You mean before she pushed you out?" Duncan didn't want to contemplate how Ivan had discovered the drive was missing, or what he might have done after.

"Exactly," Sera said. "She must have picked his pocket." She handed the thumb drive to Raphael. "I trust you can get the information off this."

Raphael tucked the device into his pocket. "As soon as we're clear of this mess."

"Did your sister say anything to you? Like why she was trying to kill you?" Trevor asked.

"She said she was sorry," Sera replied. "But I don't believe she was trying to kill me."

"Fat lot of good having the flash drive does us now," Duncan stated, fighting back the frustration building in his chest. "We have to get out of here, because there is no way we're giving you up."

"We're outnumbered," Raphael said. "Our best option is to make a run for it in the SUV."

Thankfully, they'd parked the vehicle in the garage.

"Grab anything classified and put it in the trunk," Trevor instructed. "I'll grab the computers."

"I'll help you." Jackie moved with him to unplug the laptops from the monitors.

Gunfire peppered the front of the house. Duncan tackled Sera, taking her to the floor and shielding her with his body.

Raphael moved to the front window and returned fire. "Hurry!"

Sera pushed at Duncan. He released his hold on her, rolled away and hopped to his feet. Sera did the same. Without talking, they gathered all the files that were spread across the dining table and stacked on the floor, then stuffed them into the banker boxes they'd come in and hurried toward the garage to put them in the back of the SUV.

Sera deposited the boxes she held into the back. Jackie and Trevor brought the computers and computer bags.

"We've got to move," Trevor said, rounding the SUV to the driver's side. "Where's Raphael?"

"I'll get him," Sera said and disappeared back inside.

Duncan heard the familiar buzz of the drone. It sounded like it was near the back of the house. He eased opened the back door out of the garage. Keeping to the shadows, he searched the sky and found the flying object moving in a slow circle around the house. The drone was equipped with ammunition and small projectiles. His stomach clenched. They hadn't been joking. They could bomb the house or shoot bullets from the sky. He needed to get Sera to safety. They had to make it out of this alive. Anything else was unacceptable.

Duncan ran back into the house to get Sera and Raphael. "There's a drone at our two o'clock. Trevor's waiting in the SUV. Let's move it."

Duncan witnessed Sera slip the GPS handheld device into the pocket of her jacket. She was still determined to find her sister even as their lives were on the line. He had to admire her loyalty and commitment.

Snagging Sera by the elbow, Duncan headed for the garage door. Raphael was steps behind them when an explosion rocked the house.

The deafening noise blasted through Duncan's eardrums. His nostrils flared at the bitter odor filling the air. The bright burst of flames assaulted his eyes. He ripped off the NVGs, letting them dangle around his neck. Fear for Sera clamped down hard on Duncan's heart. He grabbed her hand and pulled her through the kitchen to the back door as the fire from the missile that had been launched into the house spread, eating up the Christmas tree with hot flames.

"Raphael!" Sera broke away from Duncan and moved further into the house, clearly intending to search for Raphael.

Her panicked cry seared through Duncan. Thickening smoke filled the house and stung his lungs as he followed her. He couldn't see the ATF agent.

Duncan prayed Raphael had managed to escape to the garage. They heard the roar of an engine and a loud crash as the SUV rammed through the garage door and took off. Gunfire sounded at the front of the house. Thankfully, the SUV was armor-plated.

If they stayed in the house, they would die. Grabbing Sera's hand, Duncan shouted over the noise of the fire and the barrage of bullets slamming into the SUV. "Run!"

FIVE

Gasping for breath, Sera ran with Duncan through the rented house's overgrown backyard. Weeds and grass slapped at her legs. She breathed in the musky smells of the neglected yard to chase away the awful stench of the fire. An acre had never seemed so treacherously large.

Her heart ached. Had Raphael been trapped inside with the house burning down around him? She prayed his training kicked in and he'd escaped. She breathed deeply, fighting back the sting of angry tears as she pumped her legs harder and faster to keep up with Duncan's longer strides. He reached the back wooden fence, pivoted and, without hesitating, bent so he was in a half squat with his fingers laced together, making a basket out of his hands.

The sound of buzzing, like a hornet's nest, ricocheted through her brain. The drone that Duncan had talked about had followed them from the house.

"Up and over—quick!"

Duncan's command had her focusing. She took a running leap, one foot landing in his hands as she reached for the top of the fence. Her hand grasped the edge as he lifted her up. She vaulted her over the fence and landed soundlessly on a carpet of mowed grass in a tuck and roll. She got her feet beneath her and turned to stare at the fence. Duncan scaled it and dropped easily to his feet. A perk of being tall.

They clung to the shadows along the edge of the fence, making their way toward the neighbor's house, which was at least another acre away.

The buzzing of the drone pursued them. "We have to get rid of that thing."

"As soon as we find cover," Duncan replied.

The back porch lights of the house at the end of the long, manicured yard came on, throwing light across the expanse of lawn. An older man and woman, both dressed in nighttime attire, stepped onto the concrete pad filled with patio furniture and a large barbeque. Their terrified expressions as they watched the burning inferno in the distance did nothing to alleviate Sera's own horror and sorrow.

Please, Lord, let Raphael have made it out alive.

The elderly gentleman spotted them in his yard. He shoved his wife behind him and then shouted, "You there. What are you doing?"

"DEA Agent Duncan O'Brien," Duncan yelled out. "Go back inside and call 911. Tell them there's an agent down in the house."

The couple scrambled to go back inside, slamming the sliding glass door shut and no doubt locking it behind them.

A bullet whizzed past Sera and Duncan's heads and pierced the fence.

Shock and outrage rushed through Sera's veins. "The drone's shooting at us."

"Behind the boat." Duncan pushed her forward, using his own body as a shield as they raced to where a pleasure boat on a trailer was hitched to a big black truck parked at the side of the house. They got between the boat and the fence just as another bullet flew from the drone, embedding itself in the fiberglass side of the boat.

"See if you can unhook the trailer from the truck," Duncan told her.

Staying low, she asked, "What are you going to do?"

He removed a Glock 19 from the holster at his thigh. "Hopefully, take down that drone."

She hesitated, not wanting to leave his side. What if he was struck by one of those custom bullets? He'd need her help. They were partners. Wasn't he always saying that?

Duncan crawled under the boat, taking a position on his belly with his elbows braced on the ground and his weapon aimed at the sky. He fired several rounds at the drone. For a moment, Sera was sure he missed. Then the drone canted, as if one of the shots had winged it.

"How's that trailer hitch coming?" Duncan fired several more rounds at the drone.

Galvanized into action, she hurried to the front of the boat trailer and quickly unplugged the trailer lights attached to the truck. She undid the chains, letting them fall to the ground. She fumbled to find the safety pin holding the latch in place. She tugged it free then lifted the latch. Duncan joined her and cranked the trailer coupler off the hitch ball, releasing the trailer from the truck.

"I had it." Despite the cooler temperature of December, she wiped at the sweat dripping down her face. "Is the drone gone?"

"Yes, you did. And, yes, it flew away." He moved to the driver-side door and popped it open. "But I expect it will be back."

She moved to stand beside him. "How do you expect us to drive without keys?"

"Who needs keys?" He gestured to the truck. "Get in."

She climbed into the driver seat and reached to adjust the seat position.

"Oh, no, you don't," Duncan admonished. "Keep on moving. I'm driving."

Gritting her teeth, she debated arguing but then decided to cooperate. She scrambled over the center console into the passenger's bucket seat.

Duncan climbed in and shut the door.

"This is a newer model," she said. "Impervious to hot-wiring." She couldn't wait to see what sort of trick he had up his sleeve.

"Not when the truck has emergency roadside service available." He pushed a blue button on the edge of the rearview mirror.

A moment later, a female voice said, "Mr. Tumbler, how can I help you?"

"This is DEA Agent Duncan O'Brien." Duncan's voice filled the cab as he gave the woman his badge number. Sera liked the way he spoke with assurance, with no hint of the trauma they'd just experienced. "I need you to start this vehicle. It's a matter of life and death. Mainly mine and my partner's."

He'd claimed before they were partners. It was odd how much she liked the idea of it. But she couldn't let herself become attached to this man. Nothing in life was forever and no one stayed. Getting used to relying on Duncan, or anyone else, for that matter, would only end up hurting her in the end.

The engine roared to life. Duncan grinned and Sera couldn't help but smile back.

"We've contacted Dallas PD," the woman from the emergency roadside service company said.

"Good. Tell them to be careful. Surveillance drone with weaponry in the area."

Duncan popped the gearshift into Drive and hit the gas, pulling out into the roughly paved driveway and speeding away from the house. She stared at his profile, taking in his straight nose, the angle of his cheekbones and firm jaw. She reluctantly admired his resourcefulness as well as his handsomeness. He was cool and calm under pressure.

Not once had he hesitated in his efforts to get them away from the danger. He was going full speed ahead. But he couldn't keep this up. He must be compartmentalizing the trauma. Something she understood and did herself most of the time. Eventually, he'd crash. And for some unknown reason, she wanted to be there to help him through it.

"Where are we going?" Sera asked, hanging on to the handle on the dashboard.

"Do you have your phone?"

She retrieved it from her pocket. "I can call the US Marshals here in Dallas."

"I have a better plan," he said. "A fellow DEA agent, Sinclair James, has a place in Dallas." He rattled off the number. She put the phone on speaker.

A man's deep voice filled the cab. "Who's calling?"

"Sinclair, it's Duncan."

"Unexpected. O'Brien, what do you need?"

"A safe house. Pronto." Duncan explained the situation.

Sera marveled at the lack of emotion in his tone as he told his friend of the house fire and the drone. Her skin practically crawled with grief and anger and frustration, and every other emotion she could name. She wanted to tamp it all down. There was nothing she could do right now, and this helplessness was almost more than she could bear. She dug her nails into the palm of her hand.

Sinclair gave them an address and a code. Needing something to do, Sera quickly punched the numbers and street name into the navigation system of the truck.

"I owe you, man," Duncan said.

"I owe you much more," Sinclair said. "Stay safe."

Sinclair clicked off. The sound of the tires on the highway was drowned out by the sirens of passing rescue vehicles and Dallas PD as they headed in the other direction. Sera once again sent up a prayer in hope that Raphael had somehow managed to escape the burning house.

"You've known Sinclair a long time?" she asked.

"A decade. We've worked on several ops together."

"He said he owes you more," she said, her curiosity overriding her good sense to keep him at a distance. "What does that mean?"

For a long moment, he didn't reply. She figured she'd overstepped, telling herself his past was none of her business.

"We were in Florida. Deep in the wetlands," he said softly. "Our mission went sideways. We were compromised and walked into an ambush."

She winced. "Doesn't sound good."

"No. In the chaos, he was shot. I carried him out of the swamp and got him to a hospital."

"You saved his life." Respect and admiration flared. She liked that he didn't flaunt his heroics.

Duncan slowed the vehicle when they hit the Dallas city limits. He followed the navigation system's directions to a tall condo building in the heart of the city. He drove into the underground parking garage and punched in a code. The metal gate wheeled open and they drove through.

Duncan pulled the truck into a spot far from the elevators. He cut the engine. They made their way to the elevator.

Sera was glad when they arrived at the top floor. Inside the condo, Sera glanced around at the very masculine, homey living room, dining and kitchen space. "Is this a DEA safe house?"

"No, this is Sinclair's personal place." Duncan held out a hand. "We need to call the boss."

Sera relinquished her phone, glad to have him be the one to make the call.

Moments later, their boss, Gordon Gates, answered. "Speak."

"It's Duncan and Sera," Duncan said.

"You're alive." Sera was surprised by the note of relief in their boss's voice. "Is Raphael with you?"

Sera's heart thumped with grief. "No, sir. We don't know if he made it out. We hope Jackie and Trevor did."

"Yes, they've checked in. They are holed up at a hotel," Gordon assured them. "Where are you?"

"Still in Dallas, sir," Duncan said. "We're safe."

"Good. Stay put. I'll reach out to EMS to find out about Raphael." Gordon clicked off.

Sera couldn't help asking the question that was at the forefront of her mind. "Is there any chance Raphael survived?" She prayed the ATF agent had somehow managed to get out of the house in time.

Sadness darkened Duncan's eyes. "I pray so. He's resourceful. I won't give up hope until we know for sure one way or the other."

"We have nothing on the cartel or Ivan if the flash drive burned up." The need to move, to act, was a physical itch that drove Sera to keep going. "I need to get to my sister. She will at least be able to give us intel on Ivan and what they were after at the Fleming Investments Group."

She pulled the GPS handheld device from her pocket. The red dot was stationary somewhere north of Dallas. She zoomed in on the dot, noting the street name. Using her phone, she mapped the street. Clicking on the street view, she saw it was an apartment complex.

"Do you think you can flip her?"

"I have to try," Sera said. "She's our only lead until we know if Raphael made it out alive with the flash drive."

"Do you think you can forgive her?"

The question scored through Sera's heart. "How can you ask that?"

"It's a simple question," he said. "Forgiveness isn't

just for the person who wronged you. Forgiveness sets the forgiver free."

"I have to find her, then I can contemplate whether I'll be able to let go of the past."

He shook his head, his disapproval evident in the way his mouth pulled at the corners. "That's not the same thing."

Blood pounded in her ears. He didn't understand how hurt she'd been when Angelina left. "Leave it alone." She couldn't keep the sharpness of anger from her tone. "I don't want to have this conversation with you."

"I understand. But one day you will need to make a decision."

Her gaze dropped to the GPS unit. Not today.

"We need to eat and sleep," Duncan said, his voice firm. "It's too easy to make mistakes when running on empty. We have your sister's location. Securing her can wait while we refuel and rest."

Sera opened her mouth to protest.

He held up his hand. "You need my help. And I will give it. But we need food."

"Fine." She wouldn't admit she was hungry. Or exhausted. The combination of running for her life and the weight of anguish that Raphael might have perished was taking a toll. As long as she had a way to find her sister, Sera would exercise her very weak patience skills.

Duncan pointed to a closed door on the other side of the condo. "There's a bedroom and bath you can use to clean up."

She frowned. "I showered right before—"

He gave her his signature look with one raised eyebrow. "You might want to freshen up."

Blowing out a scoff, she headed for the bedroom. She barely glanced at the four-poster bed adorned with a green plaid comforter and throw pillows, or the dresser and sitting area, as she blew through the room to the bathroom. She flipped on the light and stared at herself in the mirror. And groaned.

Her braid was half-undone with strands sticking out in all directions. Dirt smudged her cheek. It was little wonder that Duncan had, ever so politely, suggested she freshen up.

Rolling her eyes as embarrassment heated her face, she quickly redid her braid, scrubbed her face and took a few moments to calm herself before she was ready to face him again. She found Duncan in the kitchen at the stove cooking some sort of vegetable-and-egg scramble. The scent made her stomach rumble.

Apparently, he'd also freshened up. His brown hair had been slicked back and was slightly damp, as if he'd rinsed his head. His weapon was strapped to his thigh.

Her mouth watered. She told herself it was because of the aroma coming from the pan on the stove, certainly not from the masculine and attractive man.

He caught her staring and grinned. Her stomach did a little somersault. Annoyance tamped down the attraction arcing through her. "How can I help?"

"There's water in the fridge."

Glad for a task, she opened the refrigerator to find several bottles of water. She put one on the kitchen counter for Duncan, while she took one for herself.

He lifted the pan off the flame and divided the contents of the veggie-egg scramble onto two plates. The colorful green peppers and browned onions contrasting against the yellow eggs. "Have a seat. We haven't eaten since eleven o'clock this morning. Our brains can't function without sustenance."

Her stomach rumbled, adding support to his words. She hated to admit he was right—once again. And she hated taking the time away from the job more. But the quickest way to get him to move was to eat. "Thank you."

She sat and he placed the plate in front of her. Then he handed her a fork. "Dig in."

Taking the utensil, she gritted her teeth. She didn't need him telling her what to do. Why was she always on the defensive with him? She breathed in and breathed out, momentarily closing her eyes and bowing her head to lift a silent prayer of blessing over the food and to ask God to help her rein in her impatience.

She opened her eyes and found Duncan sitting across from her with his own head bowed, his lips silently moving. Surprise washed over her. She hadn't pegged him as a man of faith, though she supposed the clues had been there.

He'd mentioned prayer before, but she had been trying hard not to pay too much attention to him. She didn't want to get attached to this man. Or anyone on the task force. Attachments led to heartache. And that was a state she avoided at all costs.

It was bad enough she'd bonded with Jace Armstrong and Brian Forrester and their respective wives. Not to mention Marshal Gavin Armstrong, and his wife, Victoria.

But even then, she held people at a distance. Her sister disappearing and then her parents divorcing had left her feeling lost and alone.

Duncan's gaze lifted, meeting hers. Attraction flared, setting off a firestorm of flutters through her system. He was so handsome. And kind and brave. He arched an eyebrow. A flash of embarrassment from being caught watching him stormed through her, no doubt darkening her cheeks.

She dove into the scramble with gusto, savoring the aromatic peppers, onions and garlic mixed with the eggs.

"Why didn't you ever mention you had a sister that went missing?"

His quietly asked question caught her off guard. She paused and carefully set down her fork. Really. He was going to go there. "It's not something that came up in casual conversation."

"We're partners," he stated. "It seems like something you should have shared."

Was that hurt flashing in his gaze? Why would he care? It wasn't as if they were romantically involved. Partners. Only in the most minimal of ways. "We haven't known each other that long."

"Maybe we haven't known each other for years. But the time we've spent has been intense," he said. "I'd like to believe you're beginning to trust me."

Was she? Trust didn't come easily for her. Too many people had let her down. Would he? Did she dare open herself up to disappointment? She was safe behind her barriers. If she didn't let anyone in, then she wouldn't get hurt. As much as she loved, respected and admired Jace and Brian, there was still a part of her she held back. Out of fear. Out of self-preservation.

After a beat of silence, he said, "Tell me about your family."

Wiping her mouth with a napkin, the rough material grounding her, Sera struggled to know where to start. Or even if she wanted to. What point was there in sharing her family's pain? But he was willing to help her find her sister. He'd gone to bat for her with their boss. He deserved to know at least the basics. "Our family was pretty typical. Dad worked in a factory as a foreman. Mom stayed home with me and Angie."

"My mom worked part-time at our local library," Duncan said. "I spent a lot of time with her there."

"That explains some things," she said. The image of him as a boy, with his nose in a book, was endearing. She would imagine he charmed all the ladies of every age.

Amusement danced in his eyes. "Like?"

"Like how book-smart you are." She'd noticed him reading on several occasions. "Maybe even why you're cautious. Hard to get hurt with your nose in a book."

His mouth quirked. "I've had my fair share of scrapes even if I was a bit of a nerd until my junior year of high school."

Curiosity overrode her good sense. She was getting too personal and attached. The seeds of trust were being planted. But would they wilt or thrive? "What changed?"

"Hormones. I grew three inches and started lifting weights. That fall, I was recruited to the football team."

"I'd imagine you had a string of girls falling at your feet," she teased. "A few cheerleaders, perhaps?"

His grin hit her in the solar plexus.

"Maybe a few. But I had a plan. College, then law

school," he told her. "I needed to keep my grades up so there wasn't a lot of time for teenage romance."

"You wanted to be a lawyer?" That didn't track with the man she was coming to know. "Don't you have a degree in economics?"

He chuckled. "I found I had a knack for numbers. It was an easier path to my ultimate goal of taking down bad guys who peddle drugs." He lifted one shoulder in a half shrug. "Plans and dreams change as we age."

"Isn't that the truth," she agreed. "I grew out of wanting to be a princess. There's no money in it. Not that being a marshal has made me wealthy. Far from it. But the job has its own rewards. Like you, my goal is to make our streets, our cities and neighborhoods safe."

They shared a smile of kinship and comradery. They had much in common—similar goals, a strong work ethic. They were both skilled at their jobs. Yet they had just as many differences that rubbed up against their similarities and caused friction. If she wasn't careful, a spark could ignite.

He cocked his head with clear curiosity in his blue eyes. "What were you like as a kid? I'm picturing more tomboy than girlie girl. But you wanted to be a princess…so what do I know?"

Amused by his assessment, she thought for a moment, then said, "Before Angelina went missing, I was precocious and adventurous. I wanted to slay dragons and wear pretty dresses while I did it. We had an elaborate tree house in our backyard that my Dad built. I defended my tree house in my pink dress and tiara, *and* brandished a sword."

The memory was bittersweet. She missed that little

girl. Acid churned in her stomach. "After Angie disappeared, I was…reckless. Getting into all sorts of trouble. I abandoned the tree house and my princess ways to get into fights at school. Lashed out at my teachers. Caused my parents headaches."

She gave a self-effacing scoff. "Mostly as a way to lessen the sting of grief from losing my sister."

He sat back with a gentle smile. "That's a very self-aware comment."

She shrugged, then told him the truth. "Mrs. Armstrong, Victoria, is a therapist of sorts. She runs a camp for at-risk youth. She helped me a great deal to understand why I push myself to excel at my job. Why I put myself in harm's way and why I have trouble asking for help."

"Jace's mom, right?"

Surprised he'd made the connection, she nodded. "The Armstrongs took me under their wing, as if I were a broken bird, when Jace and I first became friends while at the police academy. I could never repay them the kindness they've shown me. Jace is like a brother to me. He's married now and lives in Oregon."

"I'm glad you had them. Not everyone is as blessed to find others who are willing to step into our lives with wisdom and guidance. Asking for help isn't a sign of weakness, but of strength."

His words dug in deep and settled. She never liked to show weakness. "You sound like you've had someone do that in your life," she commented, hoping to direct the conversation back to him.

"I have. I'm not ashamed to admit I have sought therapy," he said, his voice taking on a sober edge. "But mostly I rely on my faith. Reading God's word. Praying. Without knowing God's love, life would be very bleak."

His words echoed ones she'd heard before from the Armstrongs. "The Armstrongs would like you."

"I look forward to one day meeting them," he said softly.

Would he? She couldn't imagine why he would meet the Armstrongs. Yet, the idea of taking him to their family ranch was inviting to her. Did he know how to ride a horse? You couldn't go to the ranch and not ride. It was part of the deal. The mental picture of Duncan in a cowboy hat, astride a horse, caused her heart to give a little leap. The thought appealed more than she cared to admit. A sinking feeling in her gut warned she was dancing too close to the edge of developing feelings for this man. And that, she couldn't allow.

SIX

"Did you and Angelina get along?"

His question brought Sera's attention back to the conversation. Back to the life she'd had when the world had made sense. "Yes and no. I looked up to my big sister, but she was…difficult. Always wanted things her way. Very moody and constantly saying no one understood her." Sera shrugged. "She was right. My parents struggled with her. I loved her but we were very different."

"I don't have siblings, but I always wanted one," he admitted. "What happened before she went missing?"

She thought back to that time. "She'd been very secretive. Wouldn't let me in her room. Hiding who she was talking to on the phone."

The hurt of being shut out still stung. "Then she started hanging around this guy named Paul…something. Don't remember his last name. My parents didn't approve. He was four years older and a troublemaker. At least that's what my dad would say. Paul worked at the tire factory with my dad. There was lots of tension between Angie and my parents. The fighting and yelling had been constant. Then one day, Angelina walked out of the house for school and that was the last time we saw her."

"Wait. What?" Duncan made a face. "She never contacted your family again?"

Sour sorrow coated Sera's throat. "No. We didn't know if she'd been kidnapped or what." Sera's stomach knotted as the heartache of not knowing what had happened to Angelina roared to the surface. "A week after she disappeared, my mom found a note that had fallen between Angie's bedside table and the bed frame."

His eyebrows lowered. "What did the note say?"

"Not much," she said. "Just that she needed her freedom."

"That's rough," he said.

Rough didn't even cover the anguish and heartbreak. "It broke my family. My parents were never the same. They divorced as soon as I graduated high school. My Dad now lives in Nevada, while my Mom moved to New Hampshire. As far away as they could get from each other and the memories of our family."

"I'm sorry you lost your parents and your sister. That's a lot of loss for a young girl."

The sympathy in his gaze had her heart thumping. "I went into law enforcement with the goal of finding Angie. I tried for the longest time. Searched every database for any mention of her or someone matching her description, both alive and deceased. Nothing. I finally accepted I'd never see her again. Until…"

"She showed up tonight at the Fleming party," Duncan said.

"Yes."

He reached across the table and took her hand. Seeing her smaller hand encased within his did something funny to her insides. Comfort radiated up her arm to circle her heart. She couldn't bring herself to pull her hand from his.

After a beat, he let go. "Tell me how Seraphina Morales celebrates Christmas."

The shift in conversation was welcome. "Work," she said. "I take the Christmas Day shift so those who have families can be with them. What about you? Do you go home for Christmas?"

"My parents escape winter in South Dakota every year from about mid-November to March. I'll see them at Easter."

"You're from South Dakota?"

"Someone has to be."

"With your movie-star looks, I'd figured you for a California guy."

A pleased expression bloomed on his face and she replayed her words in her head. Uh-oh. Did she really confess to finding him attractive?

"Thanks for that," he said. "It's not often I get such a sweet compliment."

"Don't get used to it." Time to shift the focus. "If you don't spend the holidays with family, what do you do?"

"I always look for a place to serve this time of year," he said.

Surprise washed through her. There were more layers to this man than she expected. He had depths she might want to explore. No, no—she didn't. "Serve?"

"Soup kitchens, hospitals, shelters. It depends on the city and the need."

Before she could delve into his acts of service, he

pushed away from the table. "It's late. Let's clean this up and get some sleep. Tomorrow, we'll find your sister."

As much as she wanted to protest, he was right. They needed rest. Fatigue led to mistakes. And the cost could be high. There were lives at stake, not to mention their careers. They needed all of their mental and physical stamina to perform at the highest level.

In silence, they worked together to put the kitchen back in order. Sera would have thought she'd feel awkward, or at least regretful, for talking to Duncan about her sister, but for some reason having him know the history behind her and Angie's relationship seemed important. And right.

As if he was someone she should, and could, count on.

Only because he was helping her now. There was nothing more. She wouldn't allow anything more.

The next afternoon, Duncan borrowed Sinclair's car keys. He drove while Sera navigated to the address indicated on the GPS unit. Sera held the device in her hands as if she was afraid it would disappear. She'd kept a vigil on the unmoving dot all day. Keeping her from rushing to her sister hadn't been easy, but Duncan had convinced her that waiting until they'd regrouped was for the best.

They'd touched base with Trevor and Jackie. Both were monitoring chatter on Los Campeones through the dark web, but hadn't a clue where the cartel or Ramon Vega were hiding out. They had no intel on Ivan. Until they could question Angelina, the masked thieves were a mystery.

"Angelina hasn't left the apartment," Sera told him. "Or at least the backpack hasn't."

They'd changed into clothes they'd bought at a shop near the safe house, since their clothes smelled of smoke. She'd chosen dark denim jeans and a Henley-style fleece in navy, while he'd chosen black cargo pants and a fresh black mock-turtleneck sweater. They'd wiped down their flak vests and put them on. She holstered her weapon at her waist. His was once again strapped to his leg.

He admired Sera's devotion to finding her sister. Duncan understood her need to protect her sister and bring closure to a painful part of their family's past. It was amazing to him that Sera wasn't more resentful of her sister disappearing on the family the way she had.

He was curious what Angelina had been doing for the past twenty years. Sera had to be, too. "What if your sister won't turn on this Ivan character? What if she doesn't want to be released from Ivan's hold on her?"

Fire snapped in Sera's dark eyes. "If she didn't want me to rescue her, then why did she give me the flash drive?"

"She did push you out of a helicopter," he pointed out. "Not exactly a sisterly thing to do."

"We weren't that high off the ground," Sera retorted. "If she'd wanted me dead all she had to do was wait a little longer. Or just tell Ivan who I was."

"I get that you want to save her and want to believe she'll see reason," he said. "I really do. I've been where you are. It's painful."

She studied him from the passenger seat. He resisted the urge to squirm beneath her penetrating scrutiny.

"Do you trust me enough to tell me what you mean by knowing my pain?"

His gut clenched at her softly asked question. Trusting her wasn't an issue for him. But he didn't talk about Clayton. Ever. Yet the need to unburden himself to her rose. Maybe because she'd opened up and talked about her family drama. Whatever the reason, he couldn't stop himself.

As he drove through the quiet suburban streets of North Dallas looking for the address where Sera's sister was holed up, he said, "In high school I had a friend, a football teammate, who was using anabolic steroids. I warned him using the performance-enhancing drugs would not only get him kicked off the team, but could harm him."

"Those drugs are bad news," she said.

Duncan tightened his grip on the steering wheel. "Clayton didn't want to hear it. He begged me not to say anything." Regret scratched at Duncan's throat. "I told the coach, anyway, not realizing until much later that Coach Bleeker was the one providing Clayton with the drugs. Coach was eventually arrested but by then it was too late."

"That's awful." Sera touched his elbow. "What happened to your friend?"

"Clayton found out I'd said something and cut me out of his life. If I'd only understood his behavior and the symptoms, I would have realized… He…" A deep ache pooled in Duncan's gut. "He eventually overdosed."

"I'm so sorry," Sera's voice wrapped around him, soothing the grief that threatened to rob him of speech.

"I was ignorant." The self-recrimination was a constant companion. "I should have gone to the police instead of the coach. I'll never forgive myself for not doing so."

"You were a kid," she said. "You trusted the adult to do the right thing. You're shouldering guilt that isn't yours to carry."

"My mistake has driven me to pursue a life dedicated to getting drugs, all drugs, off the street. And to putting people like Ramon Vega and his ilk, who push the drugs, behind bars." He couldn't ever forget his purpose.

"You turned your grief and pain into something productive. No one can fault you for that."

There was admiration and respect in her tone that warmed him and scared him at the same time. He had to stay the course and remember the job was the priority.

As much as he was coming to care for Sera, and despite how he enjoyed sparring with her, she was only a temporary partner. Not someone who would be in his life for long. He needed to put up a wall or he'd end up hurt when it was time for a new assignment.

Sera drummed her fingers on the dashboard as Duncan circled the block of the three-story apartment complex, located near Dallas North Tollway and Interstate 635. A wrought-iron fence surrounded the property with entrance gained through a gate controlled by an electronic keypad.

The place looked like it had once been a hotel and had been converted into apartments. An outside walkway allowed access to each apartment with stairwells at both ends of the building leading to the second- and third-floor apartments. Sera hadn't expected her sister to live in such an ordinary and humble dwelling. Maybe her life of crime wasn't so lucrative.

Duncan brought the car to a halt two blocks away. Sera checked her weapon, but before hopping out of the borrowed sedan, she turned to Duncan. "Thank you for sharing your past with me."

Her mind grappled with Duncan's story. Again, more heroics that he didn't flaunt. To be so young and responsible, and brave enough to say something when he realized his friend had a problem, was impressive. Her heart ached that his friend hadn't listened and had ended up paying the ultimate price. She was glad the coach had been stopped. And she could only imagine the betrayal Duncan had experienced.

He inclined his head but didn't look at her. "You're welcome."

She hesitated. Did he regret opening up about his friend's death? Why had he? Because she'd spilled her guts about Angelina's disappearance? She thought back to yesterday, when her world had blown up, and realized that, though she'd thanked Duncan for what he'd done for her, the acknowledgement had been grudgingly given. She wasn't that person. She wanted to properly express her gratitude. "I do appreciate you speaking up on my behalf with Gates and for helping me now. I'd be headed home with my tail between my legs if not for you. And I wouldn't have this opportunity to see Angelina again."

"Okay." He opened his door.

She frowned. Why was he acting so weird? She put a hand on his arm. "Wait. That's it? No witty quips?"

Titling his head, he met her gaze. "We have a job

to do. Your sister can get us to Ivan, who then can get us to Ramon. Why wouldn't I help you? Of course, I'd champion you to the boss. We're partners for now, remember?"

He climbed out of the sedan and went to the trunk.

For now? The words echoed through her, creating a wave of longing and sorrow. She didn't need to be reminded. He was only in her life for a short time.

Clutching the GPS tracker, she joined Duncan at the rear of the car. "Did I say something to upset you?" The words were out before she could bite them off.

Pausing, he shook his head. "Of course not."

He put on a baseball cap and a red windbreaker with a pizza company logo on the breast pocket. He handed her a matching windbreaker and baseball cap.

Deciding to take him at his word, because really digging in deep with him wasn't smart or on the agenda, she asked, "What's all this?"

"Our disguise."

His tone clearly conveyed he thought she should already know what he had planned. As if she could read his mind. The man was an enigma. Holding the windbreaker and hat, she made a face. "What exactly do you expect me to do with these?"

"One would expect that would be obvious. Put them on." He reached into the bag he'd brought from the condo and tugged out a pristine pizza box.

"We're delivering pizza?" She shrugged into the windbreaker and zipped it up. This was his plan? "Two people? Won't that look suspicious?"

"You're in training." He closed the trunk of the sedan.

Sera made a face at him as she tucked her hair under the baseball cap. "Why aren't you the one in training?"

"My idea. I get to be the lead."

Hmm. Okay, he was sort of back to his bossy self. She suppressed a smile.

As they walked up the walkway to the entrance doors, she asked, "What's in the box?"

He gave her his arched eyebrow. "What do you think is in the box?"

No way could there be a real pizza in the box. "It's empty, right?"

She liked the way he chuckled.

"Patience, young grasshopper," he quipped.

She rolled her eyes but was secretly glad to have his strange sense of humor once again in place.

He paused outside the locked gate and pushed a buzzer.

Surprised, she stepped back. "What are you doing?"

"Getting us inside the fence."

"By pushing random buttons?"

Static from the security box crackled and a man's voice answered, "What you want?"

"Pizza delivery," Duncan stated.

"Wrong apartment." The guy clicked off.

"Well," Sera said. "This is not going to get us into the complex. We should look for an open access point."

Duncan pushed another button. "Give it time."

Again, static crackled and then an elderly woman's voice said, "Yes?"

"Pizza delivery," Duncan said again.

"Oh, I'm sorry. You have the wrong apartment. It's probably those frat boys in 9A."

"Thank you, ma'am," Duncan said and clicked off. He grinned with triumph at Sera.

She gritted her teeth as her heart did a little bump in her chest at the sight of his handsome smile. "Always so smug."

"Only when I'm right." He pushed the button for apartment 9A.

Within seconds the static noise of the intercom sounded and a younger man yelled, "Hey, dude, you're late."

Duncan waggled his eyebrows at Sera as he replied into the intecom, "Sorry, dude. I got pizza."

Sera shook her head at the laid-back-surfer voice Duncan affected, just like he had when he'd confronted Ivan at the Fleming party. The man should have been an actor. But she supposed going undercover required a certain amount of acting chops.

The gate lock disengaged with a click, allowing them entrance.

They walked past an outdoor common area with stacks of lounge chairs that in summer would be scattered around the edges of the kidney-shaped pool. Umbrellas were tied down and secured. Potted plants rimmed the edges, providing a bit of greenery. There were several picnic-style tables at one end of the common space next to three communal barbeques.

Several of the apartment doors had wreaths of varying sizes and elaborate decorations. A string of white lights had been wound through the metal slates of the exterior walkway on the second and third floors. Several planted trees were lit up and had large colorful ornaments hanging from the branches.

Sera consulted the red dot and pointed to the far end

of the complex. "It has to be one of those apartments in that building."

Music floated on the slight breeze coming from apartment 9A.

As they approached the ground-floor apartment door, Duncan grabbed Sera and drew her into the shadows.

"There are two guards outside one of the third-floor apartments," Duncan said into her ear.

His breath warmed her skin and sent a shiver of awareness down her spine. His hand on the small of her back burned through the windbreaker and sweater she wore.

He urged her toward the stairwell. "Let's take the stairs."

Disconcerted by her reaction to his closeness, she said, "I didn't see them. How did you?"

The soft glow of wall sconces revealed his grin. "Super vision."

She barely contained a scoff as they hurried up the clean, well-lit concrete stairwell to the third floor. She eased open the stairwell door to peer out. At the end of the hall, standing sentinel in front of apartment 16C, were two big guys, dressed all in black.

Sera instinctively reached for her gun hidden beneath the windbreaker, but Duncan made a negative noise in his throat and whispered, "Not yet." Then, louder, he said, "Come on, trainee. See how this is done."

He stepped out of the stairwell and headed for the guards, whose gazes swiveled to them.

Staring daggers at Duncan's back, she kept a hand on her sidearm and hurried to catch up.

Duncan paused in front of the two men. "Evening. Pizza delivery."

"No one ordered pizza," the larger of the two men said in a nasally Eastern European accent.

"I beg to differ," Duncan replied good-naturedly. "Somebody called in an order for a pepperoni-and-anchovy special."

He flipped up the lid on the box, revealing it was empty, then tossed the pizza box to the closest bad guy, who fumbled to catch the flying cardboard. Then Duncan lunged for the bigger guy, tackling him to the ground.

Sera lifted her weapon at the man who'd caught the pizza box. "Don't move. Don't make a sound."

Her gaze jumped to Duncan wrestling the big guy into a choke hold. He managed to cut off his airway and render him unconscious within seconds.

She hadn't anticipated Duncan moving so quickly, so silently, or so effectively. Another dose of admiration and respect spread through her, and irritation followed closely on its heels. It was one thing to appreciate him speaking up for her and helping her, and for all intents and purposes saving her life back at the task force house, but to find herself in awe of his prowess was irksome. She didn't want to like him so much.

In a low voice, she said, "Now what?"

After he flipped the unconscious man onto his stomach, Duncan reached into his utility belt, hidden underneath the red windbreaker, and pulled out zip ties. He secured the man's arms behind his back, and then tied his feet together.

Sera tried not to notice Duncan's muscles or the grace with which he moved as he rose to his full height.

He gestured to the stairwell and said in a low voice, "Let's get them in there."

He bent and grasped the unconscious man beneath the armpits and dragged him toward the stairwell.

She shook her head, knowing all of this would be caught on the apartment building's security cameras, which hopefully weren't being monitored. She gestured with the gun for the guy still holding the pizza box to comply. The man dropped the pizza box and followed behind Duncan.

Once the stairwell door was closed firmly behind them, Duncan handed her two sets of zip ties. "Tie his hands behind him and anchor him to the railing."

"You heard the man, take a seat." Once the guard was seated with his arms behind him, Sera holstered her weapon and zipped his hands together and around the railing rung, anchoring him in place. Then she tied his feet together.

From the pocket of his windbreaker, Duncan pulled out two folded washcloths. He handed one to her.

"You thought of everything," she muttered, again impressed. He was turning out to be a surprisingly resourceful man.

"I try to be prepared for all contingencies," Duncan murmured back.

Somehow, she believed him. She stuffed the washcloth into the man's mouth.

Duncan stuffed the other one into the unconscious man's mouth before once again grasping him under the shoulders and pulling him against the railing. With another zip tie, he anchored the man's hands to the railing post. Then his feet.

"Easy peasy," Duncan said.

Though her heart thumped wildly in her chest, she said, "Well done."

With a wink, he opened the stairwell door and they walked back to the apartment, where she hoped to find Angelina. The pizza box was lying on the floor, the lid open.

Duncan picked it up and closed the lid, then lightly knocked on the door.

A few moments later, Angelina stood in the doorway, her gaze going from Duncan to the pizza box to Sera. A small gasp escaped from her.

Sera put her finger to her lips, then softly said, "Are you alone?"

Angelina stepped out to look up and down the hallway. In a low voice, she asked, "What did you do with Ethan and Petey?"

"They're alive and safe," Duncan said in a quiet tone. "Let us in."

Angelina stepped back inside, then did an about-face and walked deeper into the apartment, leaving the door wide open. Taking it as an invitation to follow, Sera kept her weapon ready at her side and entered her sister's new life.

SEVEN

Taking in the neat and tidy surroundings, Sera marveled at the fact that this was nothing like what she'd pictured Angelina's apartment would look like.

Obviously, her sister had grown into a woman who was very organized and kept a tidy home. A comfortable-looking overstuffed couch with flowered throw pillows faced a television and a bookcase overflowing with books.

Framed photos of a life that hadn't included Sera or their parents hung on the walls. The sting of hurt kept Sera from studying the images. A decorated tree stood in the corner with wrapped presents beneath. Two red-and-white stockings hung from silver holders over the gas fireplace. The reminders of Christmas knotted Sera's stomach. Finally, to be reunited with her sister, but this wasn't the jubilant reunion Sera had dreamed of.

Angelina spread her arms wide. "As you can see, I am alone." She scowled at them. "But not for long. If Petey and Ethan don't check in with Ivan, he'll send more of his men."

Sera sucked in a breath. Was she being held prisoner? "How much time?"

Angelina shrugged. "It depends on the last time they checked in. I wouldn't know." Her gaze dropped to the weapon in Sera's hand. "Why do you have a gun?"

Tucking her weapon back into her holster and ignoring her sister's question about why she was carrying, Sera said, "Ivan must have realized you gave me the flash drive."

Angelina shook her head. "No. He believes you stole it." A panicked look crossed her face. "Please, tell me you don't have it with you. If he finds you here with the flash drive, we're all dead."

A stab of concern ribboned with dread shot through Sera. Raphael had to have survived the house bombing. She hoped the flash drive had as well. "It's not here." There was no reason to confess the flash drive may be lost, burned to a crisp. That bit of information might hinder getting her sister's cooperation. "Why did you give me the flash drive?"

Angelina shrugged. "We went there to steal one account," she said, holding up her index finger. "Ivan got greedy and decided to take them all. I'd hoped you'd give it to the police."

"Was he after Los Campeones's money?" Duncan asked.

Surprised flared in Angelina's dark eyes. "No. Los Campeones's involvement with Fleming Investments Group was a huge shock."

"Then whose account was Ivan after?" Sera asked.

"Rudy Zima." Angelina rolled her eyes. "He borrowed money from Ivan to open a nightclub. When

Ivan wanted a cut of the profits, Rudy refused." She shook her head in disapproval. "Ivan found out Rudy was using Fleming to hide his money. Ivan wanted to take Rudy's money and open his own nightclub."

All this for some personal vendetta. Sera was both appalled and grateful. Without Ivan's need to get back at this Rudy guy, Sera wouldn't have crossed paths with Angelina. "Why did you push me out of the helicopter?"

"To protect you," Angelina said. "Ivan wouldn't have let you live. He thought you falling out was funny."

"Sadistic," Duncan said.

"He is that," Angelina agreed.

"What's his last name?" Duncan asked.

"Pulanski," Angelina said. "He was livid when he discovered the flash drive was missing. I convinced him you took it." She moved to the sofa and flopped down. "But he might suspect it was me. Otherwise, he wouldn't have put Petey and Ethan outside."

"We won't let anything happen to you," Sera said.

"Somehow, I anticipated you would come," Angelina said. "I just didn't expect it so soon." She gave Sera a curious look. "How did you find me?"

Duncan snagged the black backpack sitting at the end of the sofa and tossed it to Sera. Sera dug out the small circular tracking device from the side pocket. Then she tugged the GPS unit out of her jacket pocket and laid it on the table. "With these."

Angelina's eyes grew round. "You bugged me?"

"It's a tracking device with GPS. Go pack a bag," Duncan said, his voice threaded with impatience.

Angelina made a face. "I'm not going anywhere with you. Ivan would blow a gasket."

"You're coming with us, Angelina." Sera tucked the small tracker into the front pocket of her jeans. "I'd prefer it was willingly."

Angelina stared down her pretty nose and crossed her arms over her chest. The stubborn jut to her chin was so familiar it made Sera ache inside. But unlike the teenage girl she'd been, alternating between adoring her older sister and being intimidated by her, Sera wouldn't back down. She'd faced worse threats in her career and wasn't about to let her sister imagine she could get the upper hand.

"Fine. The hard way, then." Sera pulled out a set of zip ties from the other pocket of her jacket. "Angelina Morales. You're under arrest."

Angelina's eyes widened. "You're law enforcement? I should have guessed. That explains the gun and your fancy moves back at the party. What kind of cop?"

Sera pushed aside the windbreaker to reveal her gold badge attached to the waistband of her dark jeans. "US Marshal."

"Figures. You can't arrest me," Angelina protested. "You have no proof I've done anything wrong."

"Uh, I can place you at a crime scene," Sera replied. "Why are you being difficult? I'd think you'd want to get away from Ivan."

"There's no getting away from Ivan." Fear shone bright in her dark eyes. "Don't you get it? He has pull in this town. If he deems me a threat, I'll disappear."

"We can protect you," Duncan told her. "But we'll need your cooperation."

"I can't." She fisted her hands on her knees. "It's not me I'm worried about. He'll go after Grace."

The panic on her sister's face had Sera sitting down next to her and taking her hands. Back at the Fleming party, Angelina had said the word *grace* but Sera had thought she was using it as a way to ask for grace. "Angie, tell me what's going on. Who's Grace?"

Tears leaked from Angelina's eyes. "Grace is my daughter."

Stunned, Sera opened her mouth then closed it. Her gaze strayed to the two stockings. Not one for Ivan, but for Angelina's daughter. Sera had a niece? Astonishment and hurt spread equally through her chest. "Is Ivan her father?"

"What?" Angelina shook her head. "Ugh. No. Grace is twenty. I've only been with Ivan for a few years."

The information settled around Sera's heart like an anvil. Twenty. Which meant Angelina had been pregnant when she'd run away. So many questions crowded through Sera. How had Angie survived on her own? Who was the father? Paul, her old high-school boyfriend? What was Grace like? Why had Angelina run away?

All the years they'd been deprived of knowing Grace settled on Sera's shoulders. Their parents would be devastated.

Sera closed her eyes for a moment, taking the time to gather her composure. Right now, she had to stay focused on getting her sister and niece to safety. Protection detail wasn't usually her gig. But this was family. "Where is Grace?"

"Hopefully, safe in her dorm room," Angelina said. "But if Ivan realizes I'm helping the police, he won't hesitate to grab my daughter."

"Then we'll have to get to her first," Sera said.

The screech of tires outside sent a shiver of dread sliding over Sera's limbs.

Angelina jumped up and went to the window. "Ivan's here. And he's not alone. Ramon Vega is with him. This is bad. Really bad."

Angelina's words reverberated through Sera's brain like a pinball machine at an arcade.

She shared a glance with Duncan. The same concern invading her chest was reflected back to her in his blue eyes. In tandem, she and Duncan hurried to peek out the sides of the curtain.

"Yes. Very bad," Duncan agreed. "Ivan and Ramon Vega together. They've partnered up to retrieve the flash drive."

"How…?" Sera shook her head, dislodging the question. There was no time for explanations or conjecture. "We need to leave out the back."

Angelina flung her hands wide. "There is no back door."

"A window that looks out onto the back?" Sera asked, keeping her voice as calm as she could.

Unfortunately, her insides were vibrating with trepidation. No way had Ethan or Petey escaped the stairwell. Someone else could have found the guards and called Ivan or Vega. The appearance of the two men didn't bode well.

For them to team up confirmed whatever was on the flash drive could be the incriminating evidence they needed to bring down Los Campeones.

"My bedroom window faces the back." Angelina grimaced. "But it's a three-story drop."

"Not a problem." Sera was already rushing toward the back bedroom, dragging her sister along with her. The room was a surprise. Feminine in soft pinks and yellows, nothing like the dark, gothic room Angelina had made of her bedroom at their parents' house.

In the living room, she could hear Duncan moving furniture, no doubt to block the entrance.

"I have to call Grace," Angelina cried.

"No time. We'll call her when we're safe. Open the window," Sera instructed as she began stripping the bed of its flowered sheets.

Angelina gaped at Sera. "You can't seriously expect us to go out this window."

"Of course I do. Hurry."

Duncan joined them, closing the door and flipping the lock. "That's not going to hold them back for long."

Sera took the flat sheet and the fitted sheet off the bed, and began tying one corner of each sheet together. "Armoire. Angelina, window."

"Good idea." Duncan moved to the large armoire that was situated across from the bed. He opened the doors to reveal drawers and a television set. He shut the doors and turned to Angelina. "Do you have a hair tie?"

Pausing by the window, Angelina's gaze bounced between the two of them. "Am I opening the window or getting a hair tie?"

Duncan and Sera said in unison, "Hair tie."

Angelina rushed into the bathroom, then emerged a moment later with a very girlie, bright pink scrunchie band and held it out to Duncan.

He grabbed the band and stretched it around the

doorknobs of the armoire cabinet. "Help me with this, Angelina."

"To do what?"

Duncan visibly reigned in his irritation. "We're going to move it. In front of the door."

Sera rolled her eyes at her sister's obtuseness and jumped up to open the bedroom window. She popped out the screen and let it fall to the dappled willow shrubs below. She waited a heartbeat to make sure neither Ivan nor Vega had any men stationed outside the back of the building. Hopefully, they thought them trapped.

There wasn't a sound—no gunfire, no shouting—so she grabbed the sheets and lowered down one end until she was holding the remaining corner of the fitted sheet. She looked around for an anchor. The bedpost was the only viable option. She grabbed the leg of the bed, dropped down into a crouch and pulled the bed closer to the window. The wooden leg slid across the beige carpet. With quick efficiency, she anchored the corner of the sheet underneath the bedpost leg and gave a tug to ensure it held.

Duncan and Angelina managed to get the armoire moved in front of the bedroom door. Duncan nudged Angelina toward the window.

"Sera, you're down first. Then your sister," he instructed.

"Wait! I left the GPS unit on the coffee table." Sera stared at the now barred bedroom door.

"Doesn't matter. You have your sister," Duncan said.

"True." Adrenaline pumping through her veins like an open fire hydrant valve, Sera moved to climb out the window. "You make sure she gets out safely."

Duncan met her gaze, his vow to protect her sister as clear as it was solemn in his blue eyes.

Bolstered by his support, Sera slipped over the windowsill and used the sheet as a rappelling rope. She quickly made her way down the side of the building to the bushes, landing on the screen. Then she hopped to the ground, alighting soundlessly on the grass. She waved her arms, indicating she was ready for Angelina to follow.

Very slowly, Angelina sat on the edge of the windowsill, her feet dangling over the side of the building. Duncan was talking to Angelina in a low voice that Sera couldn't hear. It seemed as if he was having to coax her sister to grab a hold of the sheet, and no doubt giving her instructions on how to rappel down the side of the apartment structure. Awkwardly, Angelina gripped the sheet, twisted to brace her feet against the outside wall and slowly eased down.

Nervous energy had Sera bouncing on the balls of her toes. "Come on, come on," she muttered beneath her breath.

A loud crash broke from deep within the apartment. Sera's heart jumped and her pulse spiked. Front door? Or bedroom door?

Duncan leaned out the window and gave her a thumbs-up, indicating he was still safe. As soon as Angelina was within reach, Sera grabbed her, pulled her away from the wall and guided her feet to the ground.

"You really are brave," Angelina commented.

Surprised by the compliment, Sera didn't feel so brave as she waited with mounting anxiety for Duncan to escape the apartment. He made quick work of rappelling halfway down and then he cut the sheet with a switch-blade he'd taken from his pocket, making it impossible for anybody else to follow them. Sera's breath caught in her throat as he fell, back first, onto the bushes. He rolled off and landed on all fours.

Sera rushed to his side. "That was the most reckless thing I've seen you do."

He got up and brushed himself off. "I've been hanging around you too long."

She punched his shoulder without any heat. "I'm proud of you, though." Another loud crash from within the third-floor apartment had Sera moving. "Let's go."

Not wasting another minute, they hustled Angelina deep into the shadows of the six-foot privacy fence behind the apartment property.

"What's on the other side of this fence?" Duncan asked in a low voice.

"An alley," Angelina whispered.

"We have to climb over. I'll boost you." Duncan crouched, making a basket with his fingers just as he had when they'd escaped the fire. The man was well versed in helping others over obstacles. "Angelina, you first."

"I'm not climbing over the fence when there's a perfectly working gate right down there," Angelina said in a low, urgent voice.

Annoyance swamped Sera. "You could have said that already."

"I didn't know what you both were thinking," Angelina retorted.

At the back of Sera's mind, it occurred to her that she and Duncan seemed to read each other well, and that left her a bit off-kilter. Shoving aside the notion as something to examine at a more opportune time, she raced alongside Duncan and Angelina to the gate, which opened with a slight screech that had them all freezing like lawn ornaments. When no shout of alarm came from above, they continued. Once they were through the gate, Sera shut it softly behind them.

"We need to get to the main thoroughfare and then a cab back to our car." Duncan said.

"This way." Angelina took off at a run, heading east down the alleyway that ran between the apartment building's property and the back of a strip mall. Duncan and Sera kept pace with her. They came out onto a busy street lined with trees lit up with a ton of little white lights along the trunk and branches.

"Hey, you!"

A shout from the other end of the darkened alley sent them scurrying down the sidewalk of the strip mall to merge with the pedestrian traffic of late-night shoppers and restaurant patrons.

Duncan tapped Sera's shoulder and pointed to a restaurant. "Bring your sister."

Not questioning him, she tugged her sister to the restaurant, while Duncan pushed open the door of the Vietnamese establishment and held it while Sera and Angelina slipped past him. Once they were inside and had the door closed behind them, to Sera's astonishment, Duncan spoke in Vietnamese to the hostess and discreetly showed her his badge.

The young woman's eyes widened. She nodded and pointed toward the long counter that ran the length of the restaurant, where people sat eating. She said something to Duncan that Sera didn't understand.

"This way." Duncan walked confidently forward.

Sera and Angelina exchanged a confused look and Sera shrugged. There were many facets of this man she had yet to explore. For some reason, the thought sent a little burst of excitement through her that she quickly tamped down. She did not want to get attached to this man. But at every turn, he surprised her, which delighted and confounded her.

Duncan stopped to talk to an older Vietnamese gentleman sitting at the far end of the bar. A moment later, the man stood up and motioned for them to follow him through the kitchen. The most delicious smells swirled around Sera, making her stomach cramp and reminding her they hadn't eaten in a long time. Her mouthwatering, she stared at a bowl of noodle soup going by as a waiter passed them.

Duncan grabbed a bright blue jacket with the Vietnamese restaurant's logo on the pocket and a matching hat from a shelf near the back entrance.

The man grabbed a set of keys off a peg on the wall and handed the keys to Duncan while speaking in Vietnamese. Duncan replied, then pushed open the back door and waved Sera and Angelina through to a loading dock. A white panel van with the restaurant's logo emblazoned across the side was parked near a ramp.

"We're taking this food delivery van," Duncan said. "Get in the back and duck down."

He shrugged the jacket over his jeans and dark sweater and pulled the brim of the hat low over his eyes before he climbed into the driver seat. Sera decided to stay in the back cargo area with her sister. It was better if she and Angelina weren't seen. Ivan's men or the cartel members would be looking for Angelina.

Sera sat so she had a clear view out the front window, but was deep enough in shadow she wouldn't be seen from outside the vehicle.

After starting the well-used vehicle, Duncan eased away from the restaurant and down the street. When he turned away from the area where they had left his friend's car, Sera asked, "Where are we going?"

"Anywhere but here," he said. "There are armed and dangerous men swarming the streets."

"We have to get to Grace," Angelina insisted. "Once Ivan realizes I've betrayed him he will go after her. Please…" Angelina's voice wavered with burgeoning tears. "You can't let my daughter suffer. She's your niece, Sera."

A niece she'd never known about because of her sister's choices. The family had been broken to smithereens without a chance to love a new member. Grace. What was she like? Did she resemble Angelina? Did Grace know she had an aunt and grandparents? People who would love her, given the chance.

Bitter resentment dug in deep, but Sera pushed it away. She couldn't let herself feel, not now. She had to stay focused on keeping them alive.

EIGHT

"We'll send people to her," Sera said, though she feared it might already be too late. Sadness at the thought she might never get to know her niece swelled in Sera's chest, making her ache. She pulled her phone from her pocket, intending to call Trevor and Jackie.

"No. She knows if anybody comes asking for her to run," Angelina said. "I have to go get her. *We* have to go get her."

What had Angelina and Grace endured that running was even a conversation? Heart hurting for all the missed time and opportunity to protect and help her sister and niece, Sera thrust the phone to her sister. "Call her. Tell her to meet us in the campus parking lot."

Angelina took the phone and dialed. She waited, then winced as tears welled in her eyes. "She's not answering."

"Don't assume the worst," Duncan said. "Where will we find her?"

"Her last class ended hours ago." Angelina handed Sera the phone back. "If she's not in her dorm room, maybe she's in the library studying. She's a good girl."

Sera met Duncan's gaze in the rearview mirror. Her heart melted a little knowing he was willing to take the risk of going after her niece. She was an innocent. Saving the innocent was Sera's job. And Duncan's, even if his way of protecting the innocent was by taking drugs off the streets.

"What does my niece think of the life you've chosen?" Sera couldn't keep the anger from her tone. A child shouldn't have to live with that kind of pressure.

Angelina's gaze dropped to her hands. "She's not a fan of Ivan."

"Let's pray we get to her first," Sera said. "Step on it, Duncan."

Sera was glad to arrive at Grace's university campus without incident. Duncan parked the delivery van in the campus visitor area of the main parking lot. The lot was teaming with the sort of life that only exists on a college campus. Young adults of various ages came and went. Some driving away, leaving laughter in their wake, while others headed off in different directions. None of them paid attention to the delivery van.

The campus was lit up with colored lights and Christmas decorations. Students milled about, some wearing Santa hats, reminding Sera of the handsome Santa that Duncan had made.

Duncan opened the back doors and held out his hand.

Angelina took it and climbed out. "You're quite the gentlemen. Too bad I didn't meet someone like you."

A flash of possessive jealousy had Sera jumping from the van and wedging herself between her sister and Duncan. Her hand clamped around Angelina's elbow.

Duncan's raised eyebrow had Sera flushing with an

odd sort of embarrassment. No way would she admit to the unfamiliar sensation nagging at her.

Angelina broke from Sera's hold and started to run. Duncan grabbed her before Sera could reach her.

"We don't want to draw attention," Duncan said in a steel-edged tone.

Sera understood her sister's urgency but agreed with Duncan. "You have to trust us. We'll get to her."

"Her dorm is on the other side of the quad," Angelina said. "We should try there first."

The campus was hopping. Pockets of students hung out in various spots around the quad, which was lit up like a baseball game with huge overhead lights. Cheery garlands extended from one side of the quad to the other and colorful ornaments hung like berries ready to pick off the vine.

They made their way to the dorm building and slipped through the entrance behind a group of kids coming out. The scent of burned popcorn permeated the air, bringing back memories of Sera's own college days and the faulty microwave that seemed to always run hot. Those memories were bittersweet. She'd studied criminal justice, knowing she was headed for the police academy. She'd felt so old compared to others her age.

They took the stairs to the second floor. The overhead lights glared down on them, but the garlands hung along the walls and the glittering decorations on each dorm room door softened the atmosphere.

"Here." Angelina stopped in front of a door with an ELF poster and the names *Grace Morales* and *Kate Hempkin* spelled out with precut red, white and green letters in the shape of a wreath around the peephole. Angelina knocked. "Grace, honey. It's Mom."

No answer.

Across the hall, a trio of young women, wearing ugly Christmas sweaters, came out of another dorm room and stared at them. They appeared so young, so full of life and carefree. Sera wasn't sure she'd ever been like that.

"Who are you?" one of the young women asked as she pushed up her glasses on her small-featured face. Her sweater sported a colorful llama with a Christmas wreath hung around its neck and the words *Fa, La, Llama* in glitter-covered letters beneath the animal. Truly ugly.

"I'm Grace's mom," Angelina stated. "This is my sister and her husband."

Impressed by her sister's ability to come up with a quick cover story, Sera slanted Angelina a glance. Had she always been able to lie so convincingly?

Meeting Duncan's gaze, a warm flush of awareness shimmied across Sera's cheeks. What would it be like to call this man *husband*? Not that she was interested in him in a romantic way. Still, the more time she spent with him and came to know him, the harder it was to keep him at an emotional distance.

Giving herself a mental shake, because she had no business letting her thoughts careen down such a perilous road, Sera turned her attention to the young women. "Have you seen Grace?"

One of the girls shrugged and plucked at the pink feathers on her sweater. The motif of a pink flamingo beneath a palm tree with Christmas ornaments dangling from its beak made Sera's eyes hurt. "She went to the Alpha Epsilon frat party. It's just off campus a few blocks. You can't miss it."

"Look for the house with Rudolph on the front lawn," the last of the trio of young ladies added. Her ugly sweater had red-and-white-striped candy canes and the words *Santa Baby* in glittering red. Not nearly as awful as the other two, but still ugly. The trio hurried off, arm in arm.

"Ugh." Angelina rubbed at her temples. "I've told her a million times not to go to those frat parties." She stalked toward the exit.

"Attending a frat party is the least of our worries," Sera said as she and Duncan hurried after her sister.

"On the upside, a frat party is the least likely place Ivan or Vega will look for us," Duncan quipped.

They reached the entrance to the dorm building and just as Angelina reached for the door handle, Sera grabbed her and pulled her back. Through the glass doors, three men wearing jackets that had bulges at the hip were visible and heading toward the entrance.

"That was fast." Sera's heart hammered against her ribs. Armed henchmen were headed their way. "Ivan must've sent men immediately."

"I'm so glad she's not here," Angelina said, panic lacing her words. "Now what?"

"There has to be another exit," Duncan said.

As much as Sera wanted to get her sister out of harm's way, they couldn't chance leaving civilians unprotected. "We can't let those men terrorize the dorm."

"You're right, of course," Duncan said. "Get your sister out of here and find Grace."

What? He was willing to take on three armed goons

alone to buy her and Angelina time to get away. "I'm not leaving you. We're partners."

Not pausing to examine how easily *partner* rolled off her tongue, Sera grasped and turned the door handle of the nearest dorm room. It opened. The room reeked of sweaty socks and stale food but was empty. She shoved Angelina inside. "Stay put."

She shut the door on her sister's protest.

"Okay, then," Duncan said with a wry twist of his lips.

"Defensive positions. I'll take the right. You take the left." Sera pressed her back against the wall by the doorjamb.

"We need to do this quietly," Duncan said. "Or we'll start a panic."

"We can only do what we can do," Sera said.

If she needed her weapon, she wouldn't hesitate, but she hoped they could take the men down without discharging their sidearms. She took stock of the three men. They wouldn't be easy to bring to heel with their thick necks and bulging muscles—clearly, they all spent time at the gym. Two had hair shorn short while the third had a tousled blond mullet.

Duncan flipped off the hall lights, throwing them into shadow.

The men came in single file. Duncan hooked an arm around the first man's throat, spinning him so he faced his friends, and pulled him close to his chest. Then he gave the second guy a thrusting kick in the gut that sent him reeling backward into the third guy.

Sera took the opportunity and pounced, pushing both men out of the dorm building.

* * *

Duncan's heart slammed into his chest at the distressing sight of Sera disappearing with the two men out the dorm building's door. No way could she take on two huge miscreants by herself. He needed to get out there.

He tightened his hold on the man in his arms, willing him to pass out quickly. But the man was big and strong. The guy flung back his head, hitting Duncan in the chin. Pain ricocheted through Duncan's skull, but he gritted his teeth and tightened his hold.

With a sudden jerk, the goon twisted his torso, pushed off the ground with his legs and slammed Duncan up against the wall. The breath left Duncan's lungs in a swoosh and his hold on the man loosened slightly, enough for the guy to squirm free. Frustration roared through Duncan as he ducked a fist aimed at his face.

Not about to let this guy get the better of him and urged on by the drive to help Sera, Duncan's fist shot out with an uppercut, sending the man staggering backward. Duncan rushed forward to deliver another blow just as the dorm-room door behind the bruiser opened.

Angelina stepped out of the dorm room holding some sort of trophy in her hand like a baseball bat. She brought the large gold award down heavily on the bad guy's head. He crumpled to the linoleum floor in an unconscious heap.

"Take that," Angelina said, preparing to hit the man again.

Duncan put up a hand. "Enough. Good job." He quickly zip-tied the man's hands and feet together. "Call 911."

A grunt of pain from outside sent Duncan's heart jackknifing in his chest.

"Sera?" Angelina's cry echoed through Duncan's head.

He had to get to his partner.

The two men rushed toward Sera from opposite directions. She feigned going left but went right, and the two attackers ran into each other as she slipped away. There was something to be said for being fast, small and wiry. She delivered a swift kick to the knee of the man closest to her, sending him to the ground with a yelp of pain.

Aware of a gathering crowd of students, Sera spun toward the second assailant in time to see him reach for his weapon beneath his jacket.

Sera reached for her own, praying neither of them would fire.

But then Duncan was there, coming up behind the guy. He grabbed his arm and knocked away the weapon, then twisted the dude's arm behind his back. Duncan's other arm snaked around the man's neck in a choke hold.

Sera jumped on the back of the man whose knee she'd probably broken, then slipped her arm around his neck and pushed him to the ground. She pulled zip ties from her pocket and secured the guy's hands together.

Duncan took his opponent to the ground and did the same.

Sera grinned at Duncan. "We do make a good team."

Why did that thought scare her so much?

Sirens blared as police arrived at the scene on the campus. A gathering of students surrounded Duncan,

Sera and Angelina with phone cameras raised and recording while, Duncan and Sera lined up the suspects and seated them on the grass.

Duncan kept his head down and his back turned to the cameras. He didn't need his face flashed all over the internet. Such notoriety would make his job that much harder, especially for the next undercover assignment.

It was bad enough he and Sera were battling Ivan and his gang, but they had to deal with Ramon Vega as well. Knowing that Ivan and Ramon had joined forces to reclaim the flash drive worried Duncan. How far were the men prepared to go to get the drive back? And why had they teamed up? What terrified him most was they knew that Mrs. Claus had the flash drive. He could only hope they didn't realize Sera was Mrs. Claus.

"We have to get to Grace," Angelina insisted, the panic in her voice nearly reaching a boiling point.

"I'll deal with the police," Duncan told Sera and Angelina. "Secure Grace. I'll be right behind you."

Sera hesitated, concern darkening her gaze. "We shouldn't split up."

Was she finally coming to see him as her partner? Was she beginning to trust him to have her back? He hoped so. And as much as he wanted to stick close to her, they had to hurry. "Time is of the essence," he told her. "It's better this way."

"Right." With a slow nod, she grabbed her sister by the arm, pushed through the crowd and hurried from the scene.

Duncan was glad for the moment apart. The way she had grinned at him and declared they made a good team had his heart hitching and his breath catching. And it stirred up something inside that he had to tamp down. Longing. The need to connect. To be a part of a pair rather than be alone. How many times had he tried to forge a bond only to have his heart ripped apart?

Best not to let himself grow attached to Sera. He'd only end up hurt in the end. He turned his attention to the police officers swarming the campus. Quickly showing his badge, he drew aside the officer who seemed to be in charge to explain the situation and give his statement. "Ivan Pulanski and Ramon Vega's Los Campeones are in league with each other."

"The whole state has been trying to clamp down on Los Campeones. I've heard of Ivan Pulanski. He runs a crew, mostly extortion. Now they're colluding?" The officer shook his head. "I need to let my boss know."

The same exasperation twisted inside Duncan. But at the moment there was little he could do to remedy the situation. He needed to find Sera and her family. "If we're done here...?"

"Yeah. Leave me your contact info. I'll reach out if we have more questions."

Duncan handed the officer his card. "My cell number is on the back." He hurried away, pausing long enough to ask a student where the Alpha Epsilon frat house was located.

Once he left the campus, he turned onto the frat house's street. There was no mistaking where the party was being held. The two-story Craftsman-style house was lit up like a Christmas tree. Bright, colorful lights hung from the eaves; more strings of lights wrapped through the large lacebark elm standing in the front yard. The lawn was decorated with a blown-up Santa riding his sleigh and Rudolph with his red nose blinking on and off. Music and laughter floated out the open windows of the house.

The whole scenario brought back memories of his college days. He hadn't been one for parties, choosing to study rather than waste precious time, but he'd attended a few gatherings. He'd met his first girlfriend at a party like this one. They'd only lasted a few weeks. She'd wanted someone more attentive, and he'd been focused on graduating as quickly as possible, which meant he wasn't available to pursue a relationship.

He made his way up the porch stairs and pushed open the front door. Despite the cool temperature of the December evening, college-aged students milled about dressed in an assortment of costumes. A blond wig with braids sticking out to the sides like wings sat atop her impish face.

"Do you know Grace Morales?" he asked.

"I do," the young woman said. She gave him a good once-over. "Who are you supposed to be?"

"A minion," he said.

She grinned. "That's funny."

Reining in his impatience, he asked, "Where's Grace?"

She gestured toward the stairway leading to the second floor. "Last time I saw her she was in the den."

"Have you seen another woman dressed like me" he gestured to his body armor vest "and a woman dressed, uh, normal?" Sera and Angelina had to be here somewhere.

"Nope. Only one minion. You." She poked him in the chest. "Oh-h-h. You have a hard chest. Is that a real flak vest?"

Duncan gave a nod before slipping past her to vault up the stairs. He pushed his way down the hall, skirting a couple with flashing Christmas lights hanging around their necks.

Duncan paused to ask a much more sensationalized version of Mrs. Claus, "Grace Morales?"

"I'm Elaine," she said. "Grace is dressed like a snowman. She's in there." She pointed toward the room at the very end of the hall that had a line of people waiting to go in.

Duncan bypassed the line and headed for the door, leaving behind him a wave of protests.

"Hey, man, wait your turn."

"I was here first."

"No cutting the line, dude."

Duncan's chest tightened. He wasn't sure he wanted to know what these people were waiting in line for. He squeezed into the room. A crowd was gathered around something in the middle. He could hear the click and clack of what he recognized as a Ping-Pong ball going back and forth. Being as tall as he was, he was able to look over the heads of most of the students.

He caught sight of Sera and Angelina back in a corner arguing with a younger woman dressed in a puffy snowman costume. Both women had their arms crossed and expressions of frustration on their faces. Seeing the two women like this, he recognized the resemblance more clearly.

Duncan maneuvered his way over.

"I was winning!" Grace said. "Why did you stop the game?" She glanced at Sera and did a double take. "You are—"

Sera nodded. "Your aunt. And I wish we were meeting under better circumstances.

The screech of tires outside the house sent a shiver of dread down Duncan's spine. He moved to the window. Down below, a black SUV had roared up and parked at the curb in front of the frat house. Four men jumped out.

Duncan had a clear view as the men converged on the house, disappearing from sight. It wouldn't take them long to make their way to the second floor. He had to get Sera and her family to safety. Not out of obligation or even responsibility. But out of his growing feelings for Sera.

NINE

Heart hammering against the Kevlar vest covering his chest, Duncan said, "We need to leave. Now."

He propelled Grace with him to the window. He pushed out the screen, letting it fall onto the slanted roof, where it slid and caught on the gutter trimmed with colorful lights. "I really don't want to make a habit of leaving houses this way."

"Mom, what's going on?" Grace protested as she jerked away from Duncan's grip. "Who is this guy?"

"Never mind who he is." Angelina got into her daughter's face, grabbing her shoulders. "Ivan is after us. We have to go, or we're done for."

Color leached from Grace's face. "I told you he was bad news!"

Duncan climbed out onto the roof, thankful for the black rubber soles of his shoes gripping the tiles. "Grace."

"One sec." Grace quickly unzipped the puffy white snowman costume and stepped out of it, leaving the suit on the floor. She had on white leggings, white sneakers and a long-sleeve white tunic that fell to her knees.

He helped Grace through the window onto the roof,

then Angelina and Sera joined them. They moved to the far side of the house, away from the front entrance. A drainpipe attached to a brick column ran from the roofline to the ground.

After taking off his belt, he threaded it through the gap between the drainpipe and the column and used it to shimmy down, until his feet were on the top edge of the railing of the wraparound porch. He tossed up the belt. Sera caught it easily. "Ladies. Move it."

There was some protest above him and then Sera was handing Angelina down, so Duncan could grip her waist and lower her to the porch. Next came Grace. Much more nimble than her mother, Grace was down in a flash and barely needed Duncan's help to successfully make it to the ground.

Then Sera followed Duncan's lead by wrapping the belt around the drainpipe for leverage as she shimmied down the column. He snagged her by the waist and they both jumped to the porch. He moved them into the shadows below the kitchen window.

A few seconds later, the men who had charged out of the SUV and gone into the house came bursting out, running down the stairs to the sidewalk and looking up at the roofline. The men spread out, two moving around the opposite side of the house, while one searched in their direction. The fourth man kept vigil in front.

Keeping Grace and Angelina tucked in a crouch between them and the porch sofa, Sera and Duncan made a dark wall of protection. As the man neared, Duncan, acting on instinct and adrenaline, pulled Sera into his arms and pressed his mouth to hers.

She stiffened in his arms, but then she softened and

the kiss that was meant to distract the goon searching for them turned into something real. His heart thudded in his chest. He didn't want it to end. Time seemed to slow. The noises of the party going on around them faded.

He'd already imagined what it would feel like to hold her in his arms, but the reality was so much better. He wanted to continue to explore this new facet of Sera, this giving and soft version, but awareness rushed in as the sound of footsteps receded.

Reluctantly, Duncan broke the kiss and lifted his head to see the man turn the corner and go around to the back of the house.

Sera pushed away from him. His arms fell to his sides. They remained still, poised to react if the threat came close again. From their vantage point, they had a clear view of the men gathering in front of the house and then hopping back into their vehicle and driving away.

For good measure, Duncan and Sera waited several heartbeats before leading Angelina and Grace down the porch to the sidewalk. They hustled in the opposite direction the SUV had traveled. Keeping to the shadows of the other frat houses and sororities lining the road, they hurried around the campus and back to the front main parking lot.

As quickly as they could, they piled into the delivery van. Duncan took the driver's seat while Sera slipped into the passenger seat. Angelina and Grace sat in the back cargo area.

Hoping to delay discussing the kiss, Duncan said, "I better call Gordon." He pulled his cell phone from his pocket. Eight missed calls from Gordon. Perhaps he already had the information.

"We need Jackie and Trevor." Sera said. "I can call for reinforcements from my buddies in San Antonio." She paused. "In fact, we should head there. I know a place where we would be safe until we can arrange for something more permanent."

"Sounds good. And we can do that tomorrow. Tonight, we'll head back to Sinclair's. Food and rest." He pressed the phone number for Gordon. "We'll need to clear going to San Antonio with Gordon, anyway." The line rang. When Gordon answered, Duncan said, "This is O'Brien and Morales, sir."

"I've been trying to call your cells. Where are you?" Gordon demanded.

"We're headed to a safe house," Duncan told him. He put the phone on speaker. "Sera and I have her sister and her niece with us."

Duncan quickly explained to their boss about Ivan and Los Campeones coming after Angelina and Grace. About Angelina stealing the flash drive and putting it in Sera's apron before pushing her out of the helicopter. Duncan caught the small gasp from Grace and the way she threw her mother an incredulous look. "Ivan knows Angelina betrayed him. And Los Campeones want the flash drive."

Gordon groaned. "Having those two team up means whatever is on the flash drive is beyond dangerous. We need that drive. When Mr. Fleming came to, he told us that once Ivan moved everything onto the drive, Ivan wiped the hard drives on the computer. That flash drive is the only evidence of all that money laundering. Where is the drive now?"

Duncan met Sera's gaze. She winced, then said, "We—"

"Did you find Raphael?" Duncan asked, changing the subject. He didn't like keeping the information regarding the flash drive from his task force boss. But until they had the drive in hand again, he kept to himself the fact that it had been on Raphael when the house exploded. There was a very good chance that the flash drive had been destroyed and with it their opportunity to bring down Los Campeones's operation.

"He's at the hospital. Unconscious at present. He must have hit his head. He suffered smoke inhalation and some second-degree burns."

Duncan's stomach twisted and his heart ached for their team member.

Sera reached out and put her hand on Duncan's shoulder. "Thank God he's alive."

"I don't know if it was God or quick reflexes. He dived into the bathtub and turned the water on," Gordon said. "Jackie and Trevor are at the hospital now."

Duncan braked, then hooked a left. "We're on our way."

"What?" Sera hung on to the dashboard. "We have to take my sister and niece to San Antonio."

Duncan muted the call. "Change of plans. We need to regroup with the task force." And find the flash drive.

"You regroup. I'll take them on my own," she said.

No way was he letting her deal with protecting her sister and niece by herself against the cartel and Ivan.

"Not happening." He unmuted the call. "Sir, what hospital?"

"University Hospital," Gordon said. "I'll text you the address."

"We need to change vehicles," Duncan said.

"I'll contact the local FBI in Dallas and arrange for an unmarked vehicle for your use. They will meet you at the hospital."

"We appreciate that, sir."

Gordon clicked off.

From the back of the delivery van, Grace said, "Mom, what gives? You pushed Aunt Sera out of a helicopter? How could you?"

Duncan glanced at Sera, noting the stunned expression on her lovely face. It was probably the first time she'd heard anyone refer to her as *aunt*. And then to have Grace be outraged on her behalf must have felt good.

"Grace, it's complicated," Angelina said.

Grace scoffed. "You always say that when you don't want to tell me what's going on. I'm hungry. I want to go back to my dorm."

"No going back," Duncan said. "We can eat at the hospital."

He drove, keeping an eye out for a tail while darting glances at Sera. She stared straight ahead, her hands locked together in a tight ball. She'd yet to comment on the kiss. He wasn't sure if he should bring it up. Would she want to make a thing out it? Did he? The kiss had started as a way to hide their identities but turned into more. For him at least. But he couldn't be sure she'd feel the same. Best to act natural. No big deal, right? Sure. And he believed the moon was made of cheese.

He circled the block of the large teaching hospital several times before finally bringing the delivery van to a halt and parallel parking it on the street near the hospital entrance. He called the restaurant the van belonged to and gave instructions to the hostess as to where they would find their vehicle.

When they got out, he stuffed the keys beneath the wheel well.

And then they walked away. He prayed they could find what they were looking for.

Sera hustled her sister and niece through the hospital entrance. The automatic doors swooshed open and the antiseptic smells enveloped her, making her shudder. Thoughts pressed in on her. She'd met her niece for the first time. Grace was so much like Angelina in looks and fierce independence. Sera wanted time to get to know Grace, to discover how her sister raised this beautiful young woman on her own. What were Grace's dreams, hopes? Who was her father?

More urgent thoughts crowded in. Los Campeones and Ivan were after them and they wanted the flash drive. How far would the men go to get what they sought?

But the thought that kept rising to the surface was that Duncan had kissed her.

Kissed her!

Logically, she understood he'd done it to protect her family and that it was the right move. But still. It had been unexpected and…exciting. For a moment, she'd wanted the kiss, and the feelings it elicited, to be something real. Something more. As if they were a real couple. As if there was a future where they might end up together.

And that left her feeling like she were orbiting the earth untethered with a real threat of drifting off into the unknown universe.

And that made her mad.

Mad at the uncomfortable sprout of…hope. Mad that circumstances were out of her control.

A little voice inside her heart whispered, *God is the only one in control.*

Yes. She understood this in her heart and believed it, but still, Duncan had stunned her with that kiss and now was deviating from the plan. Well, maybe not the plan, exactly. But he had agreed that her idea of taking Angelina and Grace to San Antonio to be protected by the US marshals was a good one. She needed to get them away from the situation. Then they could work to bring down Ivan and Ramon Vega.

She understood they needed the flash drive to accomplish their task force mission. And that the flash drive was hopefully at the hospital. But the safety of her sister and niece was more important. Apparently, not to Duncan. She shouldn't have trusted him to have her back. She had to rely on herself. Giving up control wasn't an option for her. As soon as they found the flash drive in Raphael's things, she would insist on leaving for San Antonio. "Do we know which floor Raphael's on?"

Duncan gestured to a large counter area decorated with paper garland and stockings with names written in glitter. "I'll ask."

Sera held back Angelina and Grace as Duncan approached the registration desk. A moment later, he returned with a smile on his face. Her heart did a little flip. She frowned. She didn't want to be attracted to this man. He was too self-assured and confident. Which always led to problems. Men like him thought they could charm their way through life and never have to do the hard stuff.

A niggling guilt said she was wrong. He *had* done the hard thing by telling his coach about his friend's drug addiction to steroids. He dedicated his life to bringing those dealing drugs to justice and getting the nasty stuff off the streets. He was willing to help her, risk his neck for her when it could cost him his career, and possibly his life. He wasn't all fluff. But she wasn't sure how to process these new thoughts and feelings about him. And this wasn't the time to figure it out.

Duncan returned and pushed the button on the elevator. "Raphael's in room 515."

Sera and Duncan stood shoulder-to-shoulder in the elevator. Angelina poked Sera in the shoulder and gave a meaningful look toward Duncan. Sera shook her head. The last thing she needed was her sister getting the wrong idea about her and Duncan. She wasn't sure how to explain that kiss. And didn't want to. Not until she understood it herself.

On the fifth floor, at the end of the hall, Trevor, wearing khaki pants and a plaid shirt beneath a leather jacket, stood talking with a doctor in a white lab coat and Jackie, who was dressed in a navy pantsuit and a white blouse. Duncan picked up his pace. Sera hung back with Angelina and Grace.

"What's with you and—" Angelina bumped her shoulder "—tall and handsome?"

"Nothing." Sera cringed at the defensive tone in her voice. "We're colleagues."

"Right." Angelina gave her a sly wink. "The way he watches you when you aren't paying attention… And that kiss." She fanned her face. "You may believe you're only colleagues. But him…he's totally into you."

No. What her sister was suggesting wasn't true. Duncan was doing his job. He'd move on to his next assignment just like she would when they had Vega behind bars and Los Campeones was no longer distributing drugs.

Sera motioned to the chairs lined up against the wall. "Take a seat. Do not move. I'll be right back."

As she walked away, she heard Grace's voice. "She's bossy. And I'm hungry."

Sera didn't hear Angelina's reply. She didn't need to. She was sure Angelina would agree with her daughter. But Sera didn't care. Their lives were at stake. Ivan considered Angelina's actions as betrayal. He wanted Angelina to pay.

Duncan nodded at her as she stopped beside him.

"The doctor was saying Raphael could wake up at any moment."

Sera hoped this meant Raphael was recovering. "Good news then?"

"His lungs are clearing up. The burns will heal with time," the doctor told her.

Heartened to hear this, she said, "Wonderful. Can we look at his clothing?"

"We bagged everything up," the doctor replied. "His clothes are ruined and should be destroyed,"

"We need to go through the pockets of his pants," Duncan said.

Trevor and Jackie exchanged a questioning glance. Trevor cocked his head. "What gives?"

Sera exchanged a pointed glance with Duncan.

Duncan took the hint and held out his hand to the doctor. "Thank you for the good care of our friend."

The doctor shook Duncan's hand. "Of course. Let us know if you need anything." He walked away, leaving them free to talk.

Sera gave a short nod to Duncan, indicating they needed to come clean with their team.

"Raphael had the Fleming flash drive right before the house exploded," Duncan said.

"How is that possible?" Jackie asked.

"My sister stole it from Ivan and planted it in the pocket of my costume apron before ejecting me from the helicopter," Sera said. "I gave it to Raphael."

If only she'd kept it. If she hadn't taken precious moments to reveal the flash drive and pass it off, they all might have escaped unharmed. She was thankful Raphael had thought so quickly and saved himself.

Heart heavy with guilt for not having gone in search of Raphael before escaping the fire, Sera pushed open the door to Raphael's hospital room and allowed the others to enter while she remained positioned in the doorway, where she could keep an eye on her sister and niece.

Duncan headed to the closet, where he found the bag with Raphael's clothes. They were tied up inside plastic and had been placed inside a paper bag. Duncan, Jackie and Trevor went through the pockets and every inch of clothing Raphael had on him when he was found inside the house.

With a growl of frustration, Duncan shoved everything back into the plastic bag and then the brown paper bag.

He met Sera's gaze and shook his head.

Her heart sank. The flash drive wasn't here. What had Raphael done with it? How would she ever keep her sister and niece safe without it? How would they take down Vega?

This was all her fault. She had to find a way to make it right.

Duncan hurried to Sera's side, gripped her elbow and pulled her out of the room. His grip was gentle but firm. His hand warm over the sleeve of her sweater. Almost comforting. Odd. She shrugged off his hand as Trevor and Jackie joined them.

"He must've stashed the drive in the house before jumping into the bathtub," Duncan said. "Raphael wouldn't have just tossed it to let it be burned. He hid it somewhere safe."

Though Sera agreed with him, finding the drive was no longer her objective. That was his mission. She needed to get her sister and niece to safety. "Once we get Angelina and Grace to San Antonio, we can come back and search the remains of the house."

Duncan widened his stance and stared at her. "No. We search the house and then head to San Antonio."

She mimicked his posture. "I'm not risking my sister and my niece for that flash drive."

"Remember our assignment," Duncan said. "We're here to bring down a drug cartel. Ramon Vega is our quarry. We can put your sister and niece in the safe house here."

"Not happening," Sera said. "They are not leaving my sight again. I only trust my team in San Antonio."

The hurt that marched across Duncan's face made Sera's heart pound. But she steeled herself against it. This was about her family. She couldn't give in to her growing attraction to this man, no matter how much she didn't like disappointing or hurting him.

TEN

"I have an idea," Jackie interjected, drawing everyone's attention. They stood huddled together outside Raphael's hospital room, debating how best to proceed in finding the flash drive and keeping Sera's family safe.

With relief, Sera turned to the female agent. "I'm all ears."

"I say we split up," Jackie said. "I'll go with you and your family to San Antonio. Trevor and Duncan can head to the task force house to search through the wreckage."

"Not a good idea," Trevor said with a frown. "No. Us splitting up is not the answer. I agree with Duncan. Stash those two in a safe place. We do our jobs. Together."

Jackie put a hand on Trevor's arm. "You know what I'm proposing makes the most sense," Jackie said with feeling. "Once we have Sera's niece and sister out of town, where Ivan can't so easily find them, we'll head back here and be able to concentrate on the mission."

Sera jumped on the proposal. "Yes, we will. It's a good plan." She turned to Duncan. "Right?"

From the way his mouth pressed into a grim line, she could tell he was not pleased. She arched an eyebrow, daring him to protest, while at the same time willing him to agree. It was the only way they both won.

"How about you call your buddies in the US Marshals Service and have them meet you halfway," he said.

Affection unfurled inside of Sera. It was just like Duncan to come up with a compromise. She resisted the urge to hug him. Best not to give in to the growing feelings expanding in her chest. She settled for a thankful smile. "I can do that."

Seemingly satisfied, he gave a nod. She moved away to make the call just as Jackie held her hand out to Trevor.

"The keys to the SUV?" Jackie said.

As the phone rang, Sera noted Trevor didn't seem as inclined to agree to this plan. Reluctance was written in every part of his body as he reached into his pocket, then held out the keys. His fingers curled over Jackie's as she took the keys. "Do not take any chances."

She flashed him a smile. "Of course not."

Was there something going on between the two? Curiosity scratched at Sera, but now was not the time for personal queries as her friend and colleague Brian Forrester picked up the line.

"It's Sera," she said into the phone. Then she quickly explained what she needed. They agreed to a halfway point to meet.

"I'll tap Lucas," Brian said, referring to Lucas Cavendish, a newer deputy marshal. "We'll leave shortly. Stay safe." He hung up.

Grateful to her friend, she pocketed her phone and turned to find Duncan standing close. "I assume you'll let Gordon know what's happening?" she asked.

Duncan made a face. "Once I have the flash drive in hand, I'll update the boss. There's no point in upsetting the apple cart yet."

Once again, Sera wanted to hug him. Instead, she gave him a nod. "Thank you."

Jackie walked away. Over her shoulder, she said, "Come on, ladies. Let's get a move on."

Sera, her sister and her niece followed Jackie to the elevator.

"I thought we were eating here," Grace said, pushing back her dark hair from her face.

"We'll grab something on the way," Sera promised.

In the parking garage they headed for the black SUV parked five spaces down from the hospital entrance. They were almost to the SUV when a blue panel van with a sliding door rolled to a stop in front of them. Sera and Jackie flanked Angelina and Grace. Sera's heart beat in her throat. Ivan and three men stepped out of the van.

Sera gave a growl of frustration. She recognized two of the men serving as muscle standing at Ivan's side. Petey and Ethan, they had been guarding Angelina. Sera didn't recognize the third man. How had they found them?

Angelina gave a deep sigh. Sera glanced at her sister. Was that relief, irritation, or fear in her expression?

Angelina turned slightly, so that her back was to Ivan, and she stared at Sera. "Keep my baby safe."

Before Sera could react, Angelina stepped forward, holding her hands out. "Ivan, darling. Took you long enough to find me."

Beside Sera, Grace gasped, "Mom!" To Sera, she said, "What is she doing?"

Sera had to admire her sister's gumption. She was focused on protecting her daughter.

Sera turned to Jackie. "Get Grace out of here."

Jackie tugged Grace behind her and slowly moved her backward, toward the entrance to the hospital.

"But my mom," Grace protested.

Hoping to distract Ivan and his men, Sera stepped next to her sister. "You're looking for the flash drive. I know where it is. But it's not here. We can take you to it."

"Yes, you will," Ivan said and then pointed toward Jackie and Grace, who were almost to the hospital entrance. "Mateo, the girl is coming with us."

Tall, dark and lethal-looking, the man named Mateo moved toward Grace and Jackie with the automatic rifle in his hands aimed at Jackie.

Jackie pushed Grace to the entrance and pulled her weapon free just as Mateo fired, hitting Jackie in the chest. Grace screamed and put her hands over her ears as she escaped into the hospital.

Sera prayed Jackie had on a Kevlar beneath her dress shirt and suit. Grabbing Angelina by the arm, Sera pulled her down behind the nearest car.

Jackie staggered then dropped to her knees and keeled to the side, landing hard on the concrete deck.

From her vantage point wedged between two vehicles, Sera watched in horror as the hoodlum advanced on Jackie. There was no doubt in Sera's mind Mateo intended to finish the job with a bullet in Jackie's head.

Sera had to protect her fellow task force member

even if that meant surrendering herself and her sister. She sent up a silent prayer for help. Sera clung to the hope Grace would tell Duncan what Sera had said to Ivan about knowing the location of the flash drive and Duncan would realize she meant the task force house.

Duncan was their only hope of survival.

Taking a breath of strength, Sera popped up from between the cars. "Wait! Leave her alone. She's already down. We will come with you without a fight."

Ivan hesitated, his gray eyes narrowing, then he nodded. "Leave her."

Mateo paused as if considering disobeying the order, but then he turned and headed back to the van.

Sera let out a relieved breath. She didn't want anyone's death on her conscience.

Ivan said something to Petey in his native tongue. Then Petey turned to Mateo, raised his weapon and fired, dropping Mateo in his tracks.

Shock reverberated through Sera. Why had Ivan killed one of his men?

Ethan moved to Sera. "Your weapon and cell phone."

Hating to hand over her Glock, she did as requested.

At gunpoint, Sera and Angelina climbed into the van and sat on the floor as the door slid shut, throwing the interior into shadow. Musky sweat and stale take-out permeated the inside of the van and churned Sera's stomach.

Ivan sat on the jump seat and grinned at them. "Angelina, why don't you introduce me to your sister. The cop."

The unmistakable sound of muffled gunfire jerked through Duncan. "Did you hear that?" he asked Trevor.

Even as the words left his mouth, the hospital alarms sounded. Strobe lights went off and the PA system announced code silver, indicating an active shooter on the premises.

Sera!

Terror gripped his gut as he took the stairwell with Trevor hot on his heels. Pushing past others who had decided to leave as well, Duncan said a silent prayer with each step. He came out on the first floor, skidding to a halt at the sight of Grace, who was frantically talking to the hospital security guards. Dread and fear cramped his insides. Where were Sera and Angelina?

Grace gave a little cry and broke away from the guards to come at Duncan full tilt. He caught her in his arms and held her steady.

Tears streaked her face. "He took my mom and aunt. He shot Jackie."

Trevor made a distressed sound and raced past Duncan toward the exit to the parking garage.

Duncan's heart thumped hard and his stomach dropped. He released Grace. "I'll find them. Stay here." To the guards, he said, "Keep her safe." He ran out of the hospital and into the parking garage. Trevor hovered over a doctor and nurse who were tending to Jackie.

She was alive and batting away the help. "I have my flak vest on," she said. "I'm fine. We have to go after Sera and her sister."

"You might have a broken rib or two," the doctor said. "Let's get her on the gurney."

An orderly rolled a bed close.

Propped up on her elbows, Jackie said, "What? No. I don't need to be admitted."

Trevor crouched down beside her. "Do as they say, Jackie. You're injured." He smoothed back her hair.

Duncan's eyebrows rose. That seemed very intimate. A couple? For how long? Now was not the time to analyze Jackie and Trevor's relationship. His gaze zeroed in on the SUV still parked in its space. He turned to Jackie. "What happened? Where's Sera?"

"Ivan and his men took Sera and her sister," Jackie told him, concern darkening her eyes. "Ivan killed one of his..." She paused with a frown. "Where'd he go?"

"Who?" Unease slid down Duncan's spine.

"Ivan had one of his men shoot the guy who'd shot me," Jackie said. "He dropped over there. But now he's gone."

"Do you know where Ivan was taking Sera and Angelina?" Duncan pressed.

"They're headed to the task force house," Jackie said. "Sera told them she could take them to the flash drive. She could only mean the house."

Jackie tossed Trevor the keys to the SUV. When he hesitated, Duncan grabbed the keys from his hand. "Send backup." Duncan took off toward the SUV.

Behind him, Jackie said, "Go, Trevor. Don't let him do this on his own. I'm okay. I promise."

Duncan jumped into the driver seat and a second later Trevor was climbing into the passenger seat. Duncan left the hospital in a squeal of tires.

He had to get to Sera.

Shock and wariness flooded Sera as she stared at the man threatening them.

"How did you...?" Angelina's voice hitched.

"Seriously, you think I'm an idiot." Ivan shook his fist at Angelina. "It's all over social media. This female cop taking down two guys by herself. Lo and behold, it's Mrs. Claus."

Sera vaguely remembered all the cameras of the students on campus as she'd fought off her attackers. She hadn't considered Ivan would be monitoring student accounts to keep an eye on Grace. But then again, she didn't know how wide or deep his organization went. Was he part of a larger crime syndicate? Or acting independently, as Angelina claimed?

"Why did you kill one of your employees?" Sera asked.

"He wasn't one of mine," Ivan said. "He was one of Vega's snitches. Vega doesn't trust me so he had his lap dog accompany me to find the flash drive."

Sera tried to keep her shock from showing. Ivan had just betrayed Los Campeones for a second time. First by taking their accounts and now by killing one of the cartel members. There would be a price for this. She sent up a prayer that she and Angelina were nowhere near Ivan when Ramon came for his revenge.

"Why did you do that?" Angelina voiced Sera's thoughts. "Are you trying to go to war with Vega?"

Ivan sneered. "He declared war on me when he attacked our warehouse."

The man was delusional. "Did you really not know you were getting the cartel's bank accounts when you robbed Fleming Investments Group?" Sera asked.

"If I had, do you think I would've taken them?" Ivan said with a scoff. "Tell me where the flash drive is."

Her only choice was to give him directions to the

former task force house. She hoped he wouldn't realize she was taking them in a roundabout way to give Duncan time to arrive before them. "It's in the rubble left by your drone attack."

"Drone? That wasn't me. I've heard Los Campeones has gone high-tech," Ivan said with a shrug. "We'll find the flash drive. Then I'm on the next plane back to my home country. I don't need this kind of aggravation."

"What about us?" Angelina asked, gesturing between herself and Sera.

"I should kill you for betraying me," Ivan said. "I know it was you that pickpocketed the flash drive from me and gave it to your sister before you pushed her out of the helicopter. That was gutsy. But stupid."

"She didn't take it," Sera said. "I took it from you."

"Nice try. There's nothing you can say that would convince me otherwise. She got too close. And for that, she'll pay. You'll both pay."

A shiver of dread cascaded down Sera's spine. "How did you find us?" Had they been followed from the university?

Ivan reached for Angelina and took her hand. Gesturing to the large turquoise stone ring on her finger, he said, "It's so gratifying you never take this off."

Angelina snatched back her hand and yanked the ring off her finger. "I don't understand."

"I had a micro-dot tracking device embedded in the stone," he said, his grin self-satisfied.

Angelina shuddered. She threw the ring at him. "You're sick."

Ivan caught the ring and pocketed it. "It pays to not trust those close to you, Angelina. You can never escape me. You're coming with me. You're mine." He pointed at Sera. "You, on the other hand, will not be needed once I have the flash drive."

Angelina grabbed Sera's hand. Sera wanted to tell her sister to not give up hope. Duncan would realize where they were going if Grace managed to tell him what she'd said. It would be only a matter of time before help came. She just prayed that it was before Ivan decided to get rid of her.

Duncan parked the SUV two streets away from the burned-out husk of the rental house the task force had been using. He and Trevor geared up with night-vision goggles and body armor. They made their way quietly and quickly, staying to the shadows until they reached the driveway of the house. The scents of chemicals and ash made the air pungent. Surprised not to see the paneled van, Duncan checked the time. Had Ivan made a stop along the way?

Taking a position on the opposite side of the driveway from Trevor, Duncan settled his breathing. The plan was simple. Box in Ivan and his crew. Rescue Sera and Angelina with minimal shots fired.

Time crawled as they waited for the blue paneled van Jackie said had taken Sera and Angelina away. Duncan looked at his watch again. The van should have been here long before now. Where were they? Had Jackie misunderstood? Where would Sera take Ivan?

Duncan sent up a plea to God to keep Sera and her sister safe.

Remorse for agreeing to let Sera go off on her own squeezed Duncan's chest. He should've gone with Sera to take Angelina to safety, then gone to look for the flash drive. Sera was more important than the mission.

The realization tormented Duncan. He may not get a chance to tell Sera just how much she meant to him.

Sera set up a prayer asking God for inspiration and for protection. She had to trust Duncan and Trevor would get the message and be at the house waiting for them.

Ethan, driving the van, slammed on the brakes.

Sera and Angelina bounced around the back. Pain exploded in Sera's shoulder as she hit the side of the van and her teeth slammed together.

Ivan swore. "What's going on?"

"We're surrounded," Petey said from the passenger side. "Three black SUVs."

Sera's hopes soared. Dallas PD and Duncan, no doubt.

Ivan unbuckled himself and crouched between the front seats to look out the window. He swore again. "Vega. I should've known. How did he find us?"

"I see Mateo," Ethan said.

Ivan swore again. Then boxed Petey upside the head. "You were supposed to take care of that cockroach."

"I shot him in the chest. He went down," Petey whined, his accent thickening. "You wanted to leave. I didn't have time for a second shot."

"Excuses," Ivan grumbled. "Watch these two while I make nice with Vega." He opened the sliding door of the van and hopped out, shutting the door behind him.

Sera's heart thudded in her chest. Perfect. She and Angelina were smack-dab in the middle of a war between Ivan and his gangsters and the Los Campeones cartel. She went to her knees and peered out the front window, trying to ascertain where they were, but all she could see was the sky and lights from multiple vehicles. The windows on the back doors were blacked out.

She had to get her sister out of this situation. They had to survive. She had to see Duncan again. Though she didn't look forward to him gloating that he was right. They shouldn't have split up. If she'd only listened to him.

She shook her head. Recriminations and ruminating on what had already transpired wouldn't help her now. She couldn't undo the past. But she had to make a future for her and her sister. And her niece. She still hadn't wrapped her head around the fact that she was an aunt.

"You're going to let your boss go out there by himself?" she said to Petey and Ethan. "He's going to get himself killed. And then they'll kill you."

"The boss gave us an order," Ethan said, though there was doubt in his tone.

From outside the van, the muffled sounds of men arguing sent a shiver of dread down Sera's spine. The situation was bad and could only get worse. She had to do something. If she could get these two out of the van, she could jump in the driver's seat and take off.

"You better get out there," Sera said, her voice infused with a panic that should be fake, but was all too real. The longer they were here, the more risk of them being detected. "They're going to kill him. You better hurry. Ivan needs you."

Petey and Ethan exchanged a glance.

"I don't want to die," Ethan said.

"Me, neither," Petey said. "Especially not for this. I'm out of here." He opened the passenger-side door and ran, leaving the door open.

Someone shouted, "Stop!"

Then the rapid sound of gunfire shuddered through the air.

"Oh, no, oh, no," Ethan said, horror and panic lacing each word. "They shot him."

Sera's gut clenched. Poor Petey. Time was running out.

"You better surrender," Sera said, egging on Ethan. "You don't want them killing you in your seat."

Angelina grabbed Sera's arm and squeezed tight. "What are you doing? You're going to get us killed, too."

Ignoring her sister for the moment, Sera goaded Ethan. "Come on, Ethan. Stand tall. You know the only way to survive this is to get out there and draw their attention away from Ivan. Put your hands up and just get out."

Still, the man hesitated.

Raising her voice a notch, she urged, "Come on, Ethan. Get out there. Go. Go."

Ethan popped open his door, grabbed the keys out of the ignition and slowly climbed out with his hands up.

Her heart sank. They were trapped.

She grabbed the lever to the back double doors of the van and tested the lock. Secure. It would have been too much to hope Ivan and his men would be careless enough to leave the back doors unlocked. But the van was old and she doubted the lock would hold if she kicked it. She had to try. It was their only play.

She grabbed Angelina with her free hand and leaned

in close to whisper in Angelina's ear. "When I open the doors, we run as fast and as far as we can."

"What if they shoot us?" Angelina whispered back, her voice vibrating with fear.

"We have to take that chance," Sera whispered. "We're dead otherwise. No way will Ramon let us live."

ELEVEN

Sera wrenched the lever of the back doors of the blue panel van that Ivan had used to kidnap her and Angelina from the hospital. She used both feet to kick the door right at the lock mechanism. "Please, please, please," she muttered beneath her breath.

The lock busted free and the doors swung open.

With a mental fist pump, Sera scrambled to jump out of the van, her feet landing soundlessly on the pavement. When Angelina hesitated, Sera grabbed her by the wrist and tugged, forcing her to hop out. Releasing her hold on Angelina, Sera urged her forward. They ran down the narrow two-lane highway, Sera having to adjust her stride to not outpace her sister. Cold air whipped through Sera's braid and stung her lungs.

Uneasy with being so visible, Sera gripped Angelina by the elbow and pulled her off the road into the low shrubs and cacti that dotted the landscape. Not much in the way of cover, but better than out in the open, vulnerable to a bullet in the back.

Behind them, she heard shouts.

"Get them!"

"Vamos!"

"Don't look back," Sera urged Angelina as they ran.

Slipping in the dirt and grit, Sera prayed with each step Ramon would prioritize finding the flash drive over capturing them.

A vehicle approached from behind. Los Campeones searching for them? Sera tugged Angelina down behind a scraggly bush as one of Vega's black SUVs rolled passed.

Angelina gasped.

Sera clamped a hand over her mouth. "Shhh."

Holding her breath, Sera shuddered as the cartel's vehicle continued on for several hundred yards before slowly turning around and heading back the way it came. Sera and Angelina shrunk back from the edges of the headlights that touched the ground a scant two feet from where they hid. Ramon must have called his men back.

"Thank You, God," Sera breathed out.

When the bright red taillights faded in the distance, Sera said to Angelina, "Run."

Despite the cool December temperature, sweat dripped down Sera's brow and beaded on her back. Her legs burned with exertion.

The bright lights of a 24-hour diner and gas station up ahead beckoned.

Angelina slowed. "I can't… I'm out of shape."

Forcing herself to a fast walk, Sera gave in to the burning questions flooding her mind. "How did you end up with Ivan?"

"I was waitressing at a diner near where I live. He sat at my table every day for a month, before I agreed to go out with him," Angelina said between pants of breath. "He was handsome and charming." She gave a self-deprecating scoff. "I should have known better. I guess I never learn."

"Are you referring to your high-school boyfriend," Sera asked. "I assume he's Grace's father?"

"You assume correctly," Angelina said. "But he doesn't know about Grace. I didn't tell anyone. She's mine."

"So you selfishly ran away without informing him he had a daughter." Sera couldn't keep the resentment from lacing her words. "You are unbelievable. Not once have you asked about Mom and Dad."

Angelina stopped and put a hand over her heart as she caught her breath. "You were too young to realize, but Mom and Dad were headed for divorce whether I stayed or not. I wasn't going to let them decide the fate of me or my child."

As much as Sera didn't want to admit it, Angelina was right. Sera could see that in retrospect. Their parents fought all the time long before Angie ran away. It was easier to blame their divorce on Angelina's disappearance than on the fact that their mom and dad had marital problems.

"Still, you left me behind." Sera hated how vulnerable and small her voice sounded. She didn't want to be that person who needed others. But she'd needed her big sister.

Pain crossed Angelina's face. "I know. And I'm so, so sorry I did. You're right. I was a selfish, self-absorbed teenager who thought she could conquer the world on her own."

Hearing her admit it defused some of Sera's anger. They headed for the diner. "Where did you end up?"

"Galveston, at first," Angelina said. "I had enough money for a bus ticket there. Then I got a job at a hotel as part of the cleaning crew. No one asked for ID and everyone just believed me when I said I was eighteen."

As they crossed the parking lot of the diner, Sera's gaze searched for threats as she wrapped her mind around her older sister fending for herself alone. "You said 'at first'?"

"I fell in love with a guy. Jimmy," Angelina smiled, then shook her head. "Another sweet and charming man who ended up being a disappointment. He got a job on a fishing boat in Alaska, so Grace and I went with him. We broke up not long after landing in Anchorage. But I got a job at a hotel and an apartment. Grace and I were happy there."

Alaska. A long way from home. "Why did you return to Texas? Why didn't you contact us?"

"Grace wanted to go to university here," Angelina said. "I had no reason to stay in Alaska by myself. As for not contacting you, I wasn't sure anyone would want to hear from me. I burned that bridge."

At the door to the diner, Angelina put her hand on Sera's arm. "Please, forgive me for hurting you."

Part of Sera wanted to hang on to the bitterness, but she also understood that holding on to grudges corroded from the inside out. Forgiveness was a choice that would set her free of the hurt and anger.

But she wasn't there yet. Maybe one day.

They ducked inside the all-night diner. Once inside, Sera paused, assessing the lay of the land. There was a family of four in the corner. A couple of truckers sitting up at the diner counter. Two college-age women and an older woman sat in the booth near the restrooms.

The waitress paused to greet them, her hands full of meals. She had jingle bells hanging from her earlobes. A Santa hoisting a steaming mug of chocolate adorned her sweater. "Sit anywhere you like. I'll be right with you."

Sera covertly showed her badge. "Is there a phone I can use?"

The waitress' eyes widened. "There's a landline phone in the back office." She turned to face the hallway. "The employee door."

"Thank you." Sera headed down the corridor with Angelina right behind her.

The office was small and cramped, with a messy desk, an office chair and a filing cabinet. It had an exit to the back of the diner.

Sera ran straight to the landline. Punching in Duncan's cell phone number, she prayed he answered.

On the second ring, he picked up.

"This is O'Brien."

Sera had to sit down in an empty chair, because her knees turned to jelly the moment she heard his voice. An odd reaction that she didn't want to look too closely at. "Hey."

"Sera?" The urgent tone in his voice enfolded her in warmth. He was worried about her.

"Yes. Sorry. We're okay. Angelina and I are at a diner." She gave him the name and directions. "Where are you?"

"Waiting for you at the task force house. It's good to hear your voice." His relief was palpable and endearing. "What happened?"

She quickly filled him in on Los Campeones stopping Ivan's van. She explained how she and Angelina escaped.

"Smart. Stay put, we're on our way," Duncan said.

"No. We're safe for now," she insisted. "If you're already at the house, you better find that flash drive. It's the only way we'll bring down Vega."

"He doesn't matter anymore. You do. I'm coming for you," Duncan insisted.

The walls around her heart crumbled under the touching sentiment in his words and the affection in his voice. It took a second for her to grapple with wanting him to abandon their mission to be at her side. What had happened to the rule-following, focused man she'd first met? He'd blame himself if they lost this chance to bring down Vega. She couldn't let that happen. "Find the flash drive, then come get us. We'll wait here for you. Hurry."

There was a moment of silence. She smiled as she pictured him also grappling with the decision. She was rubbing off on him.

"We'll look." He hung up.

Sera moved to the small window overlooking the parking lot. If Los Campeones or Ivan showed up, she wanted to see them before they could lay eyes on her. To give her and Angelina time to make a quick exit.

After Duncan hung up, he clenched the phone in his hand. He took several deep breaths, centering his mind. Sera was safe. For now. He needed to stay on mission. The task force had been formed with one duty in mind—bringing down Los Campeones and Ramon Vega. Duncan's whole focus should be on doing the job, but his feelings for Sera were overriding his purpose. How had he let this happen?

"Sera and her sister are safe at a diner down the road. Los Campeones ambushed them. They escaped," Duncan told Trevor. "Let's see if we can find the flash drive, then get out of here."

Searching through the rubble was painstaking and dirty. The odors of burned chemicals, plastic and wood still hung in the air, making his eyes water and his lungs burn.

"So, you and Sera," Trevor said, drawing Duncan's attention.

Pausing, Duncan raised an eyebrow. His heart beat in his throat. Had Trevor somehow sensed Duncan's turmoil? "Me and Sera, what?"

Trevor laughed. "Dude, you're smitten."

Pulse skittering, Duncan tried to deflect. "Did you really just say *smitten*? Who talks like that?"

"Come on, it's just us," Trevor said. "Admit you have it bad for the deputy."

Swallowing the truth, Duncan stepped over what once was a chair. He gripped the leg and twisted, breaking it off. Using the leg to push debris around, he said, "I could say the same about you and Jackie."

"Yep." Trevor grinned unabashedly. "We've worked together for a few years. We started out as friends, but now… I'm going to ask her to marry me on Christmas Day."

Stunned, Duncan straightened to stare at Trevor. "Wow. Congratulations." A pang of envy stabbed at Duncan. "The FBI are okay with you being a couple?"

"Yes, there are some constrictions, but we'll work

with them. We make a good team, Jackie and me. Just like you and Sera."

"I don't know," Duncan hedged, unwilling to acknowledge he was falling for the pretty deputy. "We don't get along." Except when they did.

Trevor snorted. "You get along fine. All the banter is just a way for you both to keep each other at arm's length."

"Do you have a counseling degree I don't know about?" Duncan asked.

Trevor laughed. "Something like that. I've got your back."

Duncan stared at the bathtub. Water dripped from the showerhead. Raphael had bravely taken refuge from the blaze here. Duncan wanted to be brave. Brave enough to admit to his feelings for Sera. "You nailed it. I have fallen for her. But I'm not sure she feels the same."

"You won't know until you ask," Trevor said. "It took me and Jackie a while to fess up to each other. But once we did…" He shrugged. "Life made sense, you know?"

Duncan wanted life to make sense. But he wasn't sure how it could happen. "This is a waste of time. We won't find the flash drive like this. It could be burned to a crisp."

"I agree," Trevor said. "We need to bring in a working K-9 dog that specializes in electronic detection to be sure. I can make the call tomorrow."

Carefully picking his way out of the ashes, Duncan called the number Sera had called from.

"Duncan?" Sera's voice came on the line.

"We're leaving the house," he said, anxious to get to her side. "You know that saying a needle in a haystack… well, you get the idea."

"I guess that's it then," she said, her voice deflated. "Come get us. We're in the diner's office. I'll keep an eye out for you."

"O'Brien…" Trevor's voice drew Duncan's attention.

Car lights approached on the long driveway. Two big, black SUVs.

"What's happening, Duncan?" There was no mistaking the rush of concern in Sera's voice.

"We've got company." He lowered his voice as he hustled to find cover. He spotted Ramon climbing out of the front vehicle. "It's Los Campeones. Ramon."

Another man yanked Ivan out of the back passenger-side door. Headlights from the other vehicle splashed on Ivan, revealing his bruised and battered face. "They have Ivan. He looks pretty beat-up."

"You're in danger because of me." Sera's voice reverberated with self-recrimination. "I should've listened to you."

"No time for that now. Get to Sinclair's apartment. You'll be safe there. Trevor and I have to get out of here." Duncan clicked off.

Duncan withdrew his Glock from its holster and prayed he and Trevor managed to get out of the situation alive.

Sera gripped the phone in her hand, trying to process what had just happened. The disappointing news that Duncan and Trevor couldn't find the flash drive was eclipsed by the horrifying reality that Ramon was there. No way would Duncan and Trevor survive. They were outmanned and outgunned.

Beneath her breath, she said, "Oh, Lord, please. Don't let anything bad happen to them. Help us. Help us all."

Duncan and Trevor needed backup. Pronto. Sera called the task force headquarters number. Within moments, Gordon was on the line. Telling him the truth of the situation wasn't easy. To her surprise, he didn't reprimand her, but promised to send reinforcements to Duncan and Trevor's location and a car to pick up her and Angelina.

"Thank you, sir," she said. "We'll find a way into the city. I'd rather all law enforcement resources were directed to Duncan."

"Don't thank me yet," he said. "You and your sister need to get to a safe location."

"We will, sir." Somehow, she would get Angelina to Sinclair's apartment.

Her next call was to Brian. He and Lucas had reached the halfway point. The options were to wait for them at the diner, or find a way to get to Sinclair's apartment and meet them there. The idea of waiting made her skin itch.

Headlights cut across the parking lot as a black SUV turned in. Sera's breath caught. It wasn't the task force's vehicle.

Los Campeones had arrived. Ramon must have sent his men looking for them again.

There was no choice now—they needed to leave ASAP. Spying a trucker crossing the parking lot to his big rig, she gave Brian the address and the security code for Sinclair's apartment.

"Be careful," Brain insisted.

"Always," she replied and hung up. "Come on, Angie," Sera said. "We have to get out of here."

Cautiously, she opened the back door. A few cars were parked behind the building. Most likely the employees. For a half second, Sera thought about getting the keys and commandeering one of the vehicles, but that would require going back inside the diner, where Vega's men would soon be.

Instead, she and Angelina hustled across the parking lot, keeping to the far edge until they reached the trucker.

"Excuse me, sir," Sera said. "We need a lift into the city."

"Sorry, darling, I'm headed in the opposite direction," the man said as he climbed up onto the step of the door to the cab.

"It's a matter of life and death," Sera replied, putting steel in her voice. She reached for her badge.

Angelina let out a frustrated sigh and put a hand on Sera's arm. "That is not the way to deal with people, Sera. You get more flies with honey than vinegar." She nudged Sera aside. "Sir, what's your name?" Angelina asked in a very charming voice that had Sera raising her eyebrows.

"Calvin," he replied. "And what's yours, sweetheart?"

"Calvin, I'm Angie, this is my sister, Sera. You seem like a nice man." Her voice dripped with honey. "We're in a bit of a jam. You see, it's very important I get back to my daughter. She's in Dallas and in danger. You're our only hope. Please. You'd be our Christmas hero."

Sera barely contained a scoff. Her sister's words seemed to work, though.

Calvin rubbed his chin, then said, "All right. How could I refuse to be a Christmas hero? I'll make a detour. Only because you asked nicely." He glanced at Sera. "You could learn a few things from your sister." He opened the door to the rig. "Hop on in, ladies."

Angelina flashed Sera a smug smile before she hustled around to the passenger side of the cab. Following, Sera had to admit her sister was a force to be reckoned with. They had to share the front passenger seat. Sera buckled the seat belt over both of them.

"This thing is strangling me," Angelina said, plucking at the strap.

"Too bad." Safety was paramount in a situation like this. If Ramon tried to run the big rig off the road, they needed to be strapped in.

"Okay, ladies, hold on to your hats. Here we go." The big semitruck started up with a deep rumble and moved slowly out of the parking lot of the diner. Sera kept an eye on Vega's men. Two of them stood inside the diner, then disappeared down the hallway that led to the employee office.

She'd made the right call to leave.

Duncan's heart rate sped up and adrenaline flooded his system. He and Trevor hunkered down behind the remains of what once was the dining table. He could see Ramon and his men approach the front of the house.

Trevor tapped Duncan on the shoulder and gestured to the back of the house. Nodding, Duncan moved in a low crouch out the remains of the back sliding door behind Trevor. They made their way around the side of the house. They'd left their vehicle a half mile down the road.

There wasn't much in the way of cover between where they were hiding, behind a recycle bin, and the road.

"We make a run for it in three," Duncan said.

Trevor acknowledged with a chin nod.

"One, two, three," Duncan counted in a low voice.

They both lunged to their feet and ran.

Bullets zipped past. A searing pain ripped through Duncan's upper right bicep, spurring him to move fast and to pray for all he was worth.

Lord, please put a hedge of protection around us!

Sera paced the living room of Sinclair's apartment. Angelina sat on the couch watching her. Her friends, Brian Forrester and Lucas Cavendish had arrived ten minutes ago. Brian had one hip leaned against the counter separating the living room from the kitchen, while Lucas had taken a position by the window.

"Would you stop pacing? You're making me dizzy," Angelina said. "Your man will be here when he gets here."

Sera's heart thudded. Her man. No, no, no. Duncan was not her man. Yet, she couldn't help the worry gnawing at her insides. That last phone call, hearing his hushed words saying Ramon had arrived, had sent fear sliding down her back. Why hadn't he called to give an update?

Were he and Trevor okay? Were they lying in a pool of blood at the house? Had Ramon taken them hostage?

Done with this helpless feeling and the anguish crowding her chest, she turned to Lucas and Brian. "One of you needs to take me to the house. The other one take Angelina to the hospital to be with Grace and Jackie."

"Not happening, Seraphina," Brian said. "We're waiting here for the rest of your task force. Then we will make a decision on our next move. You might as well get some food and rest."

"Just for the record," Angelina said as she moved to the kitchen, "Grace and I are not going into WitSec."

Sera fisted her hands. Her sister was so stubborn. Ever since Sera had brought up the possibility of entering the program, Angie had balked. "I told you it's the safest way to keep you and Grace out of Ivan's clutches."

"That's no kind of life." Angelina put her fists on her hips. She looked at the two men and then Sera. "I can't ask Grace to give up everything. Not for me, not for Ivan." As if done with the conversation, she said, "Anyone want a sandwich?"

Barely containing a growl of frustration, Sera hoped to scare some sense into her sister. "But we've learned the hard way people connected to organized crime manage to orchestrate violence from behind bars."

"You heard Ivan." Angelina pulled peanut-butter and a package of sliced bread from the cupboard. "He wants me to go with him when he leaves the country." She opened a jar of jelly and began making the sandwiches. "He has no intention of hurting me. I'm more afraid of being killed by Vega and his men." She handed out the sandwiches.

Sera took the offered food. "You have good reason to be afraid. Los Campeones will hurt whomever they deem deserves it."

"Can you put Ramon Vega behind bars? You did that with Garcia." Angelina took a bite of her own sandwich.

Angelina was right. They needed to put Ramon Vega and his cartel out of commission. And the only way to do that was to get the flash drive. Which brought her around to her initial request. "I need to go to the house. We need to make sure that Duncan and Trevor are okay. We need to search the rubble again. If the drive survived the fire, we need to find it. It's the only way to take Vega down."

"Let me touch base with the Dallas PD," Brian said. "They may have information on your two task force members. If the house is secure, then we can talk about going there."

Reining in her impatience, Sera forced herself to eat. The salty and sweet taste burst on her tongue and satisfied her hunger.

An hour later, the buzz of the security system on the door to Sinclair's apartment disengaging sent Sera's heart rate skyrocketing. She grabbed Angelina and dragged her to the back bedroom, then told her sister to stay put and shut the door. Because Ivan had taken her weapon, Sera grabbed the nearest object at hand. A fire poker.

Strange to find one in the apartment considering the fireplace was gas. The poker seemed lighter than normal. She inspected the poker and realized it had a twist-off handle. She unscrewed the gold-colored round end and removed a long blade attached to the knob.

Now this, she could work with. Interesting item for Sinclair to have. Was he a weapons nut or just paranoid? Holding the weapon down at her side, she stood ready. Lucas and Brian took defensive positions.

The door swung open to reveal Trevor and Duncan. Both men were grimy with soot and ash, a clear sign that they'd been searching for the flash drive.

Duncan held a bloodied cloth to his bicep. His gaze locked on to her. "Are you okay?"

"Me?" Both irritated and flummoxed that his first question would be about her welfare, she hurried to his side. "You're hurt!"

TWELVE

Sera's pulse skittered and a knot of dread formed in her gut. She led Duncan to the couch and made him sit. She undid the Velcro straps of his Kevlar vest and helped him out of the heavy tactical gear. Glancing at Trevor, she said, "You should've taken him to the hospital."

"He wouldn't go." Trevor ran a hand through his messy hair. "He insisted I bring him to you."

Her heart contracting painfully in her chest, Sera stared into Duncan's blue eyes. "What happened?"

"After I hung up with you, we were able to hide, but they spotted us making a break for the SUV. Ramon and his men shot at us, but we managed to escape."

"I didn't realize until we were here that he'd been hit," Trevor said. "He hadn't said a word."

"Sounds about right." Sera wanted to shake Duncan. "And you call me stubborn."

He arched an eyebrow. "What can I say? I've learned from the best."

She wasn't sure if she wanted to throttle him or kiss him. She did neither. They had an audience. Best to tamp down her emotions and stay focused on the situation. She didn't need Lucas or Brian reporting back to Marshal Armstrong that she was acting unprofessionally.

"I'm calling the hospital to check on Jackie and Raphael." Trevor moved to the entryway for privacy.

Sera looked up at Lucas and Brian. "Lucas, can you tell my sister it's safe to come out of the bedroom, please. I'm sure she's anxious to know what's going on. Brian, would you please grab some clean washcloths and some water? I need to see where all this blood is coming from and dress the wound." She put her hand over Duncan's on the cloth covering his arm. "Let's take a look."

He curled his fingers around hers. Her gaze lifted from his wound to his eyes, so soft and full of affection. Her insides fluttered.

"I like this side of you," Duncan murmured. "Very nurturing."

Embarrassed by both his words and her reaction to him, she muttered, "Don't get used to it." Returning her attention to wiping at the blood still seeping from his arm, she said, "You've lost a lot of blood."

He relaxed back against the couch cushions. "I'm fine. It's just a graze."

Arching an eyebrow, she said, "So you're a doctor now?"

His grin was lopsided and so charming. "I've done a stint undercover as a doctor."

She barked out a laugh. "Of course, you have. You have an answer for everything."

"Not everything." He closed his eyes with a grimace. "We didn't find the flash drive."

"Instead, you found a bullet." Guilt pricked her. If she'd stayed with him instead of letting herself and Angie get kidnapped, he wouldn't be injured now. "I'm sorry."

"Not your fault," he said. "Don't take on underserved guilt."

Easy for him to say. He was the one bleeding.

Brian handed her a stack of washcloths and a bottle of water.

Duncan's eyes darkened. "They have Ivan and one of his men."

A gasp from behind Sera had her turning to see her sister standing with her hand clutching her throat. "Is Ivan dead?"

Duncan shook his head. "I don't know. Last time I saw him he was alive, but hurt."

Angelina moved to the armchair and sat down heavily. "I don't know why I am so upset by this. I wanted him out of my life. But not hurt or…dead."

"You're upset because you're a good woman at your core," Duncan said. "And we don't know if he's dead." He met Sera's gaze. "Anyone who would put the health and welfare of their daughter over themselves is good people in my opinion."

Sera had to agree, and she liked Duncan more for saying so. He was good people. Kind and compassionate. Decisive and courageous. A man to count on. Butterflies took flight in her chest.

Boy, she was in trouble.

To distract herself from the connection arcing between her and Duncan, she held out a hand to Brian. "Knife?"

Without hesitation, he slid a knife from a leather

sheath strapped to his ankle and handed it over. She cut the lightweight mock-turtleneck sweater away from the wound. After rinsing the injury with the bottled water, she used a clean cloth to wipe away the blood oozing out. The wound was in the soft meaty tissue of his left biceps. A graze, just as Duncan had said.

"There's a first-aid kit in the trunk over there." Duncan pointed with his good arm across the room.

Lucas went to the trunk and opened it. He whistled softly. "There's a nice assortment of firearms here."

After taking the kit Lucas offered from the trunk, Sera removed a gauze bandage and wrapped it around Duncan's wound. Though he tried to hide it, she noticed him wince.

She shook her head, marveling at his obstinate refusal to show pain. "It's okay if you want a groan or scream. That has to hurt."

He gritted his teeth. "Don't want you to think less of me."

Rearing back, Sera opened her mouth to protest when Angelina handed Duncan a sandwich. "You need to keep up your strength."

"Thank you." With his uninjured hand, he took the offered food and ate it in three bites.

When Trevor walked back into the living room, Angelina gave him a sandwich as well. "You're a lifesaver." He gobbled down the food, then wiped his mouth with a napkin and said, "Jackie has two cracked ribs. Raphael is awake. And Grace is crawling up the walls, itching to get back to campus."

Sera wrapped Duncan's wound in more gauze from the first-aid kit and tied it off with a square knot.

Blood immediately began to seep through the layers. She grabbed a clean washcloth and affixed it over the gauze with more gauze. "You're going to need stitches."

"I need to get to my daughter," Angelina said.

"I'll take you," Trevor said.

"We will all go," Duncan said.

"Agreed," Sera said. "You need to have that arm looked at. But you need to change your shirt. Where will I find a clean one?"

Duncan gestured to the bedroom. Sera hurried into the room and found a button-up dark flannel shirt hanging in the closet. She also grabbed Duncan a dark weatherproof jacket.

After helping him dress, she armed herself with a SIG Sauer from the stash of guns in the trunk. She slipped an arm around Duncan's waist as he rose from the couch. There was a question in his eyes, but then he smiled and leaned into her. He probably didn't need her help, but she was giving it, anyway.

She caught the looks that Lucas and Brian sent her and threw one back at them. She wasn't going to explain herself. Especially when she wasn't sure what she was feeling or thinking. Duncan had squirmed under her skin in an unfamiliar way. It was both thrilling and disconcerting. But nothing could come of allowing herself to fall for him.

Fall for him?

Where had that thought come from?

She was not falling. No falling to be had here.

No, sirree.

But as she held him close to her side, a surge of affection and awareness of him as a man had her tightening her arm around his waist as they made their way to the parking garage.

Lucas and Brian headed to their unmarked SUV. Normally, Sera wouldn't have thought twice about riding with them. They were her friends and colleagues. But right now, she was part of the team with Duncan. Partners. She needed to stay dedicated to him and the task force. Getting him to the hospital to have his wound looked at was a priority.

She and Duncan climbed into the back passenger seat of the task force SUV. Trevor drove while Angelina sat in the front passenger seat. Sera was thankful for the backup of her colleagues.

At the hospital, Angelina rushed to Grace's side, and they immediately began quietly arguing. Angelina was well aware of what was at stake. She wouldn't let her daughter go back to campus yet. None of them would be safe until they brought down Ramon Vega and Los Campeones.

Addressing Lucas and Brian, she gestured to her sister and niece. "Would you two mind keeping them safe?"

"Of course," Lucas said. "We have your family. You see to your partner."

She couldn't even form a protest at their use of the moniker linking her and Duncan. They were linked. A bond had formed without her realizing it. At some point, she was going to have to deal with her feelings for the man, but not now.

"Excuse me," she said to the nurse at the desk, showing her badge to expedite the process. "Agent O'Brien has been wounded and probably needs stitches."

"Let's get you into an exam room." The nurse whisked him away to have his wound cleaned and stitched up.

It took all of Sera's willpower not to go with him. But he didn't need her hovering while the medical professionals did their jobs. Shoving her emotions for Duncan into a box for later examination, she made her way to the fifth floor.

She was not surprised to find Jackie and Trevor were already in Raphael's room, keeping him company. Jackie, wearing a hospital gown covering her bandaged ribs, occupied the one chair in the room while Trevor hovered close, her hand held tenderly in his. If Sera had had questions before about whether these two were involved, they'd now been answered. There was no mistaking the tenderness and intimacy between them.

Something akin to envy throbbed in Sera's chest. It was the same sort of sensation she'd experienced when Jace had married Abby, and Brian had married Adele. Sera had stood up for both of her colleagues during their weddings. She'd resigned herself to always being the odd one out. The fifth wheel.

Was it too much to hope that might change with Duncan in her life?

Propped up in the bed, Raphael said, "There she is." Though bandages covered various parts of his hands, arms and shoulders, he was smiling. "Where's your partner?"

Glad to see him awake and alive, Sera approached Raphael's side. She was getting used to the moniker. She and Duncan were partners. But for how long? There was the rub. The thing that would keep her from allowing him fully into her life. He'd leave just like everyone else. "Duncan will be along soon. He's getting stitched up. He got in the way of a bullet."

"Not too serious, I hope," Raphael said.

"Not too." She patted a place on Raphael's shoulder that wasn't bandaged. "You gave us a scare. We thought you were right behind us when we escaped the house."

"I scared myself," he replied. "I *was* behind you, but then a wall of fire cut off my escape. I made it to the bathtub, though." He held up his bandaged hands. "It could have been much worse."

"Yes, it could have," she agreed and sent up a praise to God for answered prayers.

"Where are we on the case?" Raphael asked.

"Vega is still on the loose," Trevor reported. "He's on the hunt for that flash drive. He believes we still have it. But we can't find it."

"What do you mean you can't find it?" Raphael asked. "Did something happen to the SUV?"

Sera's heart raced. "Other than it took heavy fire, it's intact. Why?"

"I tossed the flash drive into one of the computer bags Jackie was carrying out."

Which meant they'd had the flash drive the whole time.

"Thank you," Duncan said to the nurse who finished stitching up his wound. The bullet had cut a path through the muscle in his upper arm. He now sported four stitches beneath a tight new bandage, with more bandages in a bag and instructions on how to care for his wound. Thankfully, the bullet missed any major arteries. But he'd have a scar.

He pulled on the shirt Sera had grabbed from Sinclair's apartment. He was anxious to see her. To let her know everything was okay with his arm. But to be honest, it was also just to see her. To assure himself she was okay. There was so much for him to say.

Admitting to himself that he'd fallen for her was huge. Admitting it to Trevor was monumental. Did he dare admit it to Sera?

Would it be better if he held off until the task force completed its mission? He'd never been in a situation like this one before. Unsure how to navigate his feelings and his job, he headed out of the ER exam room and made his way up to the fifth floor. He was sure he'd find Sera with Jackie and Raphael.

It frustrated him that they couldn't catch a break in their pursuit of Los Campeones. They needed to stop Ramon. To stop the drug trade. That goal was his life's purpose.

Time to regroup. They needed to talk Angelina and Grace into going into Witness Protection for the time being and then the task force could get back on track. Duncan had to stay focused on his purpose. So how was he going to hide his feelings from Sera? It was definitely going to take a lot of acting skills on his part, but he could do it. He had to.

Sera pushed the button for the elevator that would take her to the parking garage. She had the keys to the SUV in her hand. She couldn't believe they'd had the flash drive this whole time somewhere in the back of the SUV. Excitement revved through her veins, along with messy emotions where Duncan was concerned.

She searched her heart and lifted up a prayer, asking God to reveal the truth. Her heart hammered against her rib cage. She stepped inside the elevator and the doors slid shut. Her reflection stared back at her. She always tried to be honest. Tried to be truthful even when it might be painful. What were her feelings for Duncan? She cared about him. More than cared. Had she fallen for him? As in…love?

Maybe. It was so foreign and strange to feel this deep connection and affection that seemed to spread through every cell of her being. Is this how Jace and Brian had felt when they realized they loved their wives? She'd have to ask them.

As the doors opened on the parking garage, she gave herself a mental shake. Her feelings were inconsequential at the moment. What mattered was getting her sister and niece to safety, and securing the flash drive so that they could complete their mission.

It was time to shore up her defenses around her heart. Falling for Duncan would only lead to sorrow. There was no future for them. He was DEA, always on the move, looking for the next assignment. Once this task force was dismantled, she would go back to San Antonio, back to her team. Back to her life. Now her best play was to find the flash drive and be the professional that her boss expected her to be.

She headed to the SUV that Trevor had been driving. The sides were pockmarked with bullet holes. She shuddered at the reminder of the danger that lurked. She pressed the button to release the locking mechanism. The SUV's lights came on and an electronic chirp sounded, echoing off the concrete walls of the parking garage.

From around the back end of the SUV, Ramon Vega and his sidekick, Mateo, stepped into view. The two men couldn't have been less alike. Where Ramon was short and square, Mateo was lanky and towering.

Sera's heart stopped. Then pounded in gonglike fashion as the word *run* screamed through her mind. As she reached for the weapon she'd taken from Sinclair's apartment, she pivoted, intent on escaping back into the hospital, but strong arms grabbed her and held fast. More men stepped out from behind cars.

A man to her left took the SIG Sauer from her hand, but she wasn't defenseless. No way would she go down easily.

She stomped on the instep of the guy closest to her, on the right. She sent an elbow into the guy on her left. He grunted and doubled over, yanking her to the ground. She fell to her knees, and pain ricocheted up her thighs and into her stomach. She tried to rise but heavy hands on her shoulders kept her on her knees.

Was this how she would die? A soul-searing anguish flooded her veins. There was still so much for her to do. For her to say. To Duncan. To Angelina.

Sera regretted not offering her sister forgiveness when she'd asked.

Ramon stopped in front of her. He was wearing a leather bomber jacket zipped to his chin. His dark hair and even darker eyes pierced her. "Well, well, aren't you a feisty one? Deputy Morales, I want the flash drive. Give it to me and I'll let you live."

"I don't have it." She wasn't about to tell him they

were within feet of the flash drive. It was the only leverage they had and the only way her death would have any meaning. "Killing me won't get you it."

Ramon studied her for a long moment. She kept her expression as neutral as possible, hoping the panic and fear zipping along her limbs wasn't visible. She should've waited for Duncan, or accepted Trevor's offer to accompany her to the parking garage. But she was a US marshal. She didn't need anyone.

She could hear Duncan's voice in his head saying her stubborn willfulness would get her in trouble one day. Today seemed to be that day.

Needing someone wasn't a sign of weakness. It was a lesson taught to her by Duncan. One she should have heeded. Would she see Duncan again? Grief stabbed at her mind and her heart.

"I believe you're right—killing you won't get me what I want," Ramon said. He gave a chin nod to one of his minions behind Sera. "Bring her."

Fully intending to make it difficult for them to get her up and moving, Sera braced herself for the fight. But the blow to the back of her head was unexpected. Pain exploded deep throughout her skull. The lights of the parking garage dimmed to a pinpoint.

Her last thought before the lights winked out was a prayer that Duncan would bring down this man and exact justice. For her. For them all.

Duncan entered the hospital room where Raphael was lying in one of the beds, awake and talking with Jackie and Trevor. Sera, her sister and niece and the other US marshals were nowhere in sight.

"Man, it's good to see you alive," Duncan told Raphael. Although seeing the bandages covering the burns Raphael had sustained made Duncan wince. He'd never suffered more than a sunburn and thought that was painful. He couldn't imagine how much worse second-degree burns would hurt.

"You as well, brother," Raphael replied.

"Jackie, how are we feeling?" Duncan noted that Trevor held Jackie's hand.

After hearing that Trevor was going to ask Jackie to marry him on Christmas Day, Duncan could only smile at the sight of the obvious affection between the two. Apparently, they'd decided to no longer keep their relationship status a secret.

"I'm good," Jackie said. "I really don't need to be here. I should be helping you and Sera."

"Speaking of Sera, where did she and her family go?"

"The deputies took Angelina and Grace to get food," Trevor said.

Duncan frowned. "Sera didn't go with them?"

"No, she didn't. She went down to the parking garage," Trevor said. "Get this. Raphael, here, tossed the flash drive into one of the computer bags as Jackie passed him in the hallway as we were leaving."

"Seriously? Good job. Way to protect the evidence," Duncan said. He wished they'd known sooner. But at least the flash drive was still in play. "How long ago did Sera leave?"

"Five minutes, max. I offered to go but she wanted to go on her own." Trevor gave Duncan an encouraging nod. "This would be a good time for you to—"

Duncan made a strangled sound and held up a hand. "Stay out of it."

"A good time for him to do what?" Raphael asked. "Do spill."

Duncan shot a daggered look at Trevor. "I have your back. You have mine?"

Trevor nodded. "Of course. Sorry. It's nothing."

"Not nothing," Jackie said. "He and Sera have feelings for each other. It's so obvious."

"Obvious? No, it's not." Even to his own ears, Duncan's protest lacked conviction.

Jackie smiled. "We get it. But fighting the inevitable only wastes time."

As much as Duncan didn't want to admit it, Trevor and Jackie were both right. This would be a good time for him to see Sera alone for a moment, not that he was going to tell her of his growing feelings yet. There would be time for that once they were out of danger.

He just wanted to make sure she was okay. To be near her. Okay, truth be told, he was tired of fighting off the love growing in his heart.

Wow, he'd actually attached the *L* word to his feelings.

Swallowing back the trepidation that realization caused, he paused, then said, "I'll be back."

Suddenly anxious to see her, Duncan took the stairs down to the garage. He came out on the opposite end of the task force SUV. The sight that met his eyes had his heart jumping to his throat and panic rearing like a wild mustang.

Sera was being lifted into the trunk of a dark green sedan. Her head lolled to the side. Clearly, she was unconscious.

Terror squeezed the breath from Duncan's lungs. He ran forward as he reached for his Glock strapped to his leg. He fired at Ramon. The man dove into the sedan. The car backed out of the stall.

Afraid to fire any more rounds into the sedan for fear of hitting Sera, Duncan raced after the vehicle. It burned rubber through the parking lot as it sped away. Duncan chased after the sedan as fast as he could but there was nothing he could do to stop them from kidnapping Sera, except note the license plate number. The car exited the parking garage onto the main street and merged into traffic.

The concrete ground felt as if it was dropping out from under Duncan's feet. He let out a primal scream of rage and agony. He couldn't lose her.

THIRTEEN

Adrenaline-fueled, Duncan raced back into the hospital, his feet pounding on the stairs to the fifth floor. His chest heaved with panic, tightening his lungs and squeezing all the air out, leaving them shriveled like grapes left too long in the sun. As he came to the floor where Raphael and Jackie's room was, the two US marshals held up their hands. They blocked the hallway, standing side by side. Both tall. One dark and one light. Both dressed in denim and cowboy hats.

"Whoa, slow down," Lucas Cavendish said.

"Where's the fire?" Brian Forrester asked.

Duncan skidded to a halt. His throat closed, trapping his rage and terror. The fear pounding in his brain kicked into overdrive and forced words past the lump of dread choking him. "Sera. She's been kidnapped. Ramon Vega."

"Tell us what happened," Brian barked out.

Trevor stepped out of the room and Duncan waved him over. The image of Sera being loaded into the trunk of the sedan played on a loop in his brain. He would never be able to erase the shocking scene from his mind.

"Ramon took Sera. He's in a dark green sedan. I memorized the license number. We have to find her." Horror skittered across his flesh, raising goose bumps on his skin. "She was unconscious."

What had Vega done to her? Was she alive? If so, for how long? Where would Vega take her? Why had he kidnapped her?

"Did she have the flash drive?" Trevor asked.

"I don't know." He should've checked the SUV. But his only thought was to get help for Sera. They were wasting time. They needed to mobilize and find that sedan.

"I'll check the SUV." Trevor took off. Then he abruptly stopped and turned to face them. "She had the keys. We'll have to break into the vehicle."

"I'll call DPD and get them on the surveillance cameras in the area." Lucas moved away, already dialing the phone

"I'll tell our boss. We'll tap into the marshal services resources." Brian moved away to talk on his cell.

Duncan's hands fisted at his side. How were they going to find her? Dallas was a huge area with many ways in and out. Highways that would take them all the way to Mexico. Or north through the middle of the country. Where would Vega feel safe enough to stash a US marshal? Vega had to know that every law-enforcement agency from the west coast to the eastern seaboard would be hunting for him and search for her.

"Agent O'Brien?" Angelina said as she and her daughter stepped out of the public restroom. Her expression clouded at the sight of him. She looked around with a frown. "Where's Sera?"

Anxiety was a living, breathing dragon inside of Duncan. He was afraid if he opened his mouth he might let loose with a blast of blame toward Sera's sister. None of this would be happening right now if Angelina hadn't reappeared in Sera's life. If she hadn't hooked up with Ivan. If she hadn't run away, leaving Sera hurt and alone.

He gave himself a mental slap. This wasn't anyone's fault but Ramon Vega's. He was the villain here. Unable to sugarcoat the situation, he said, "Ramon took her."

Angelina gasped and tears welled in her eyes. "Oh, no."

Grace placed a soothing hand on her mom's arm and asked Duncan, "How are you going to find her?"

"What about the tracker? The one you used to find me?" Angelina asked. "She put it in the pocket of her jeans."

"Of course." Why hadn't he thought of that. Because his brain had frozen the second he'd realized what was happening to the woman he loved.

The problem was the GPS unit that would tell them Sera's location was still at Angelina's apartment on the coffee table, where Sera left it. He could only hope it hadn't been destroyed, stolen or run out of battery.

He quickly explained to the US marshals and Trevor.

"We have to get that GPS unit," Lucas said.

"We can't leave Angelina and Grace unprotected," Duncan said. "Sera would never forgive any of us."

"They can stay with me," Jackie said from the doorway. She'd pulled on a jacket over her hospital gown covering her bandaged ribs. Her blond hair hung loose over her shoulders.

"Jackie, you are supposed to be resting." In two long strides, Trevor was at her side.

She gripped his arms. "My ribs are broken. Not my hands or my head. I can shoot and I can think. Find my weapon and I will keep Angelina and Grace safe."

Grateful to the FBI agent, Duncan turned to Angelina. "I need you both to stay here with Jackie. Do not leave. Do not make this harder for Sera than it already is."

Angelina reached out and put her hand on Duncan's good arm. "You find my sister. But be careful. You're injured. She would hate it if something worse happened to you."

Duncan wasn't so sure the sentiment was true, but it was nice to hear. After making sure that Angelina and Grace were ensconced in the room with Jackie, who now had her weapon at her side, Duncan led the way to the parking garage. Lucas and Brian peeled off to retrieve their vehicle while Duncan and Trevor headed to the task force SUV. It was unlocked. Trevor popped the trunk hatch.

Duncan grabbed the closest computer bag and searched the bottom. He found a silver flash drive as well as a red one and a blue one. "Found it."

"I found it," Trevor said almost at the same time, and held up two silver flash drives and a white one.

"The colored ones aren't it. But hang on to the silver ones. One of these has to be the incriminating evidence that will put Vega behind bars," Duncan said.

The US marshals rolled up in their SUV.

"Get in," Lucas said from the driver's side.

Brian sat in the front passenger seat.

Duncan and Trevor slid into the back passenger seats. After giving Lucas directions to Angelina's apartment, he fought to keep the anxiety from overwhelming him. Why had Sera been so stubborn as to not let Trevor accompany her to the parking garage?

Trevor had grabbed a laptop from the SUV. He powered up the computer. "Let's see which of these flash drives is the right one."

He plugged in one drive and opened the contents. Spreadsheets from the task force investigation into Los Campeones appeared on the screen. He clicked out and tried the next one. Surveillance photos of Los Campeones appeared.

Duncan stared at the images of Ramon Vega while acidic rage burned in his gut. He silently vowed to make the man pay for touching Sera. For taking her away from him. If Vega hurt her... His thoughts careened down a dark path of scenarios that ripped gapping wounds in his soul.

Despair danced at the edges of his consciousness, but he wouldn't let it step fully into his mind. He clung to his faith, to the hope that God wouldn't let Vega harm Sera. But Duncan was well aware that sometimes God's answer to prayers wasn't the wanted answer. He swallowed back the rancid taste of bile inching up his throat. "Let's try the last one."

Trevor traded out the flash drives. The drive held a single file labeled *Fleming Investments Group*. "Pay dirt."

Heart hammering at his ribs like a woodpecker attacking a tree, Duncan asked, "Can you copy the file?"

"Already on it," Trevor replied. "Though, what's the

likelihood that Vega hasn't already moved all of his money?"

Duncan's chest knotted. "He may have, but he still wants the file badly enough to kidnap a US marshal, so there has to be some value to it."

"Maybe he's just a thief and wants to steal the money from other accounts?" Lucas said from the driver's seat.

Duncan's blood turned to molten fire. He flexed his hands and rolled his arm, testing the stitches. He had to be ready. He couldn't let anything deter him from rescuing Sera. "Whatever the case, the man is going down."

At the apartment complex, they quickly gained access by showing badges to a resident on his way out.

Duncan hurried to Angelina's third-floor apartment, the other men hot on his heels. The door had been busted open, the hinges now mangled. Inside the apartment, furniture had been upended as if in a fit of rage. The Christmas tree had been knocked over. The ornaments broken, and pieces scattered across the floor.

Both of the stockings that had hung over the gas fireplace were turned inside out and discarded. Apparently, Ramon and Ivan had searched for the flash drive without any regard to the damage they were doing to Angelina's apartment.

The bedroom door had been kicked in. The large armoire that Duncan and Angelina had pushed in front of the door was now face down on the carpet.

The GPS unit wasn't on the coffee table in the living room. Shaking with adrenaline-fueled dread, Duncan dropped to his hands and knees to search for the unit. He found the device underneath the couch. A moment of triumphant relief made him drop his forehead to the carpet.

He flipped on the unit's power button, sent up a prayer of thanks it still held a charge and a red dot blinked at him.

Hope swelled at the tentative connection to Sera. He zoomed in on the location and relayed the information to the others.

Lucas called the local US Marshals Service, as well as the Dallas PD, giving them the location. The four men raced back to the SUV. Lucas fired up the engine and they took off.

Duncan sent up another desperate prayer, asking God to watch over Sera. "We're coming Sera. We're coming," he muttered beneath his breath.

Sera woke to shivers racking her body. A damp coldness breathed across her neck. A foul musty odor assaulted her senses. A throbbing headache from the blow she'd sustained to the back of her skull had her wincing. She attempted to reach up to touch her scalp, but her hands were duct-taped to a chair. She assessed her surroundings. Drab gray walls with signs of water damage from a leak in the low ceiling. No other furniture aside from the chair she was strapped to. A cold concrete floor. A door about four yards away. She was trapped in what appeared to be an empty storeroom. A high window behind her provided natural light. How long had she been tied up in this room? It was clearly daytime.

She was alive. That was something. Other than the agonizing headache, she was intact and unharmed.

Movement behind her sent her heart racing and a different sort of chill skated across her flesh. She wasn't alone.

Twisting her neck, she tried to see behind her but was unable to.

"Who's there?" Using her unbound feet, she managed to scoot the chair sideways enough to see a person lying prone on the floor, facing the wall.

A groan sounded. Masculine. Her heart thumped. Duncan? A stab of fear tore through her.

No, he was safe at the hospital. Ramon had some other prisoner here with her.

"Hey," she said. "Hey, you! Wake up."

Another groan. The man slowly rolled from his side to his back. Sera could make out his profile. Surprise buffeted her. Ivan.

Astonishment gave way to irritation. This man had caused her and her family so much grief. "What are you doing here?"

Ivan turned his head and met her gaze. His face was battered and bruised. Lips cuts, eyes swollen. "I'm a prisoner, like you."

As much as she believed he deserved to be behind bars, empathy for his pain twisted her chest. Vega and his men had really worked Ivan over. "Are you tied up?"

He lifted his bound hands. At least he didn't appear to have broken bones. His surface injuries would heal. But he could have sustained internal damage that might still do him in.

"Can you move? I need you to make your way over to me," she said. "Even with your hands bound you can pluck this tape off of my wrists. Then I can get us out of here."

"I should be on a plane to home right now," he said, self-pity infusing his words. He didn't budge.

Annoyance chased away her empathy. Why was he being difficult? "If you want to get to your home country then you need to help me so we can escape. That's the only option."

"He'll never let us go," Ivan said. "He's going to kill us. Make an example out of us. Anyone who crosses Los Campeones will die." He said the last part with a strange attempt at mimicking Vega.

Gritting her teeth, Sera worked to calm her frustration. In an even voice, she said, "We have to make sure that doesn't happen."

"What are you and I going to do?" Ivan scoffed. "We have no weapons. We are bound and stuck in this room."

His fatalistic tone grated on her nerves, intensifying the intense pulsing in her skull. "Help me get this duct tape off my wrists," she insisted with steel in her tone. "You're alive now. Stop acting like you've already died."

He let out a defeated sigh. "But we're as good as dead."

She rolled her eyes at his self-pity. "Are you always this pessimistic? I don't know what Angelina was thinking when she got mixed up with you."

"Angelina. My angel." Ivan's tone softened. "She's the only good thing that has come out of being here in Texas. I didn't want to come here. But I had no choice at the time."

The man was really getting on Sera's last nerve. Why would he want to return to his home country if his life would be in danger there? The man made no sense. She played on his feelings for Angelina. "If you want to see my sister again, then you've got to help me."

"She left me."

"Come on. If you care about Angelina, you'll fight for her. Where's that bravado you had at the Fleming party? Was it all just show? You're only brave with a gun in your hand?"

He turned away from her, curling into a ball like a pill bug.

She stomped her foot with aggravation to get his attention. "Hey. I need you to get over here. Now. Move it."

With another deep, soul-weary sigh, Ivan slowly worked himself to a sitting position. His ankles were bound together as well. On his backside, he inched his way across the floor to her side. He lifted his bound hands to use his stubby finger to tear at the tape. "You wouldn't, by chance, have a knife on you?"

Was he trying to be funny? "I wish." When she got out of this situation, she was going to get a Ka-Bar knife and ankle sheath like the one Brian wore. Too bad she hadn't kept the weapon when she'd borrowed it earlier.

Ivan made little headway ripping the tape. While he worked on her left wrist, she bent forward, hoping to tear the tape on her right wrist with her teeth. But she couldn't quite reach it. Frustration, anger and dread folded over her like a heavy blanket. Was despair contagious?

Noise at the door had them both stilling.

Her pulse skittered.

"Get back to your corner," she urged Ivan. If Vega found him trying to help her escape, they might both end up dead.

Ivan didn't hesitate. He scooted quickly back to the corner. He'd just made it when the door swung open. Ramon Vega and his sidekick, Mateo, walked inside.

Mateo moved straight to Ivan and kicked him hard in the gut. "You're going to die."

He grabbed Ivan by the arm and yanked him to his bound feet.

"Don't do this," Sera said. "Don't add murder charges to your rap sheet."

Ramon held up a hand to stall Mateo.

Mateo growled. "Don't listen to her. He tried to kill me. If I hadn't had body armor on, he'd have blood on his hands."

"We all have blood on our hands," Ramon said. "But for now, leave the man. We'll deal with him in good time. Right now, I need her cooperation."

Mateo thrust Ivan back to the floor. He landed with a thud and a yelp of pain. Sera winced.

"I look forward to cutting you up into little pieces," Mateo said.

Sera suppressed a shudder. The malice in Mateo's voice wasn't for show.

Ramon stepped forward with a flip phone. No doubt a burner that couldn't be traced. "Call your buddies and tell them to bring the flash drive to me in exchange for you."

"They don't have it," she told him. "It was burned up in the house you bombed."

"I don't believe you," Ramon said. "There were two agents at the house. They found it. I know it."

"But they didn't find it," Sera insisted, telling him the truth.

"Then I might as well just kill you now." Ramon pocketed the flip phone and reached for the weapon at his waist. He aimed at her head.

Staring down the barrel of the SIG Sauer she once possessed, Sera swallowed back the bile burning its way into her throat. She wasn't ready to die today. Not when there was a chance that Duncan might still be able rescue her. She needed to give him every possible moment to find her. "I'll call him. But you have to untie my hands."

"You don't need your hands to talk," Ramon said. He tucked the gun back into his waistband and brought the flip phone out from his pocket again. "Number?"

Gnashing her teeth and knowing she had no other choice, Sera gave him Duncan's number. Ramon put the phone on speaker.

"O'Brien."

Duncan's voice filled the storage room. Sera nearly wept with a longing so deep and an ache so wide it threatened to swallow her whole. "It's me—Sera."

FOURTEEN

Sera's voice filled the interior of the US marshals' SUV. Duncan's heart contracted painfully in his chest as relief swept over him like a cool breeze. They were speeding across town toward the location the red dot indicated. Maybe she was hiding. He prayed she was somewhere safe. "Are you okay? Did you escape?"

"She is unharmed at the moment." Ramon Vega's voice came on the call.

Duncan flinched. Dread strangled him. For a moment, he fought for breath. A rush of rage filled his veins like lava bursting from a mountain. If that man hurt her…

"She did not escape," Ramon continued. "But she will die if you do not bring me the flash drive."

Duncan debated denying having the flash drive. But Sera's life was on the line here. He would do nothing to endanger her more than she already was. "I'll bring it to you. Just give me your address."

"Not so fast," Ramon said. "We'll call you back with the location. You better not be yanking my chain. I'm not a dog for you to play with. She will get a bullet between the eyes if I don't have that flash drive by the end of the day."

The line went dead.

"We're twelve minutes out from the location," Lucas said.

Duncan clutched the GPS unit, praying harder than he had in his whole life. *Please, Lord, please.* He wanted to spend Christmas with Sera. He wanted to spend the rest of his life with her. They just needed a chance.

Ramon walked out of the storage room, shutting the door behind him and Mateo.

Sera didn't have the luxury of dwelling on how good it had been to hear Duncan's voice. Or that he was in a vehicle. She could hear the tires on pavement. Where was he headed? Had he remembered the tracking device in her pocket? She wasn't even sure the small disc was still on her.

"Get over here," Sera barked at Ivan. "Keep working on the tape."

"Your people did have the flash drive all along," Ivan said. He grudgingly inched his way back over. "I knew it."

The knot in her gut tightened. "Apparently so."

But would Ramon honor his word and let her go once he had the drive in his possession? Or would he kill them both? What had Ivan said, that Ramon would "make an example out of them to anyone who dared cross Los Campeones?"

Dread seeped into her limbs, making her shiver again.

Would she see Duncan again? The thought of dying without telling him how she loved him created a well-spring of sorrow that threatened to bubble up and choke her. She blinked back scorching tears. No. She wouldn't give in to despair. She needed to cling to her faith, just like Duncan had talked of. She had to cling to the hope that God would see her through this ordeal, and that there would be a way for her and Duncan to have a future together.

"We have the building surrounded," the SWAT commander for the Dallas Police Department said. Duncan, Trevor, Lucas and Brian had just arrived at the staging point, across the street from the warehouse where the tracker indicated Sera was located.

"Have your people hang back while we go in," Duncan said. "Detain anyone who tries to escape."

Turning to Lucas, Brian and Trevor, Duncan instructed, "You three go after the targets Ramon and Mateo. I'll secure Sera."

The two US marshals exchanged a glance. "Just what is your relationship with Sera?"

Fully cognizant that Sera considered Lucas and Brian to be her brothers she never had, Duncan didn't blame the two men for wanting to protect her. He wanted to appease them and reassure them, but now was not the time for him to delve into his emotions.

He needed to stay focused. Detached. They all needed to come home safely.

Dressed in borrowed DPD tactical gear, Duncan adjusted the assault rifle strapped across his body. "Good question. One I'll address when we have Sera back, okay? Let's roll."

They approached the warehouse in a two-by-two formation. The building looked worn and in need of repair. Several windows were broken out. No lights shone inside. But looks could be deceiving. Was Ramon using this place for his illegal activities? Or was it just a place for him to stash Sera? They reached the steel door. Duncan gave a nod. Brian tested the handle. It turned easily in his hand. A shiver chased down Duncan's spine. Why wasn't the door locked?

"Look for trip wires," Duncan said. He'd been in situations like this before. If it seemed too easy, there was always some unseen danger waiting to take them out.

Brian pushed open the door and used a flashlight to search the edges of the doorframe and the entryway for wires leading to explosives. "Clear."

They breached the warehouse. Duncan and Trevor went to the right, Brian and Lucas to the left.

The building was cavernous. And empty. High windows allowed light to stream in, revealing a single table set up in the middle of the vast space.

"Clear," Duncan said, unable to keep the frustration out of his voice.

"Clear," Brian echoed. "There's a storeroom where she might have been. A chair with discarded duct tape. Drops of blood on the floor."

Anguish speared through Duncan, making his vision swim and his muscles jump. Was the blood Sera's? Had Ramon lied when he said she was unharmed? Cautiously, Duncan approached the table. Sunlight glinted off Sera's badge. Next to it was the small round tracking disc. Defeat slumped Duncan's shoulders. Now how were they going to find her?

The only option was to wait for Ramon to call again.

"He's toying with us," Lucas said.

"To what end?" Duncan's fingers wrapped around Sera's badge, the edges digging into his flesh.

"A game only he knows the rules to," Brian stated.

The jingle of Duncan's cell phone jolted through him. He fished the device out of his pocket. He hit the answer button and then the speaker. "Who is this?"

"Nice try, DEA Agent Duncan O'Brien." Ramon's voice sounded tinny through the phone in the cavernous space.

"Where is she?" Duncan could barely contain the tide of anger surging through his blood and coating his tongue.

Ramon tsked. "You have the flash drive with you?"

Stifling a growl, Duncan said, "I do."

"Then head to Klyde Warren Park," Ramon instructed. "You alone. Stand behind the Christmas tree. I'll find you."

"Let me talk to Sera," Duncan insisted, unable to keep the edge of panic from his voice. "I have to know she's okay."

There was the sound of shuffling and then Sera's voice came online. "Duncan, I'm all right. He hasn't hurt me."

Relief to hear her voice liquified his limbs. He steadied himself on the table with a hand. "Sera, you can count on me. I'll get you out of this."

"I know I can count on you," she said, her voice soft and filled with an emotion that created an ache in Duncan's chest.

"Duncan, in case things go sideways," she said. "I want you to know... I love you."

Duncan's heart tripped over itself. His tongue seemed too big for his mouth. Heat crawled up his spine. "I—"

The line went dead.

Had she really just told him she loved him? Was that some kind of code? Or was it real? He tried to call the number back, but it was already disconnected. There was no way to trace where the call had originated. A dead end.

Brian let out a whistle. "Never thought I'd see the day when Sera fell in love."

"We will get her back safely," Lucas said, his voice razor-sharp.

"And when we do," Brian said, giving Duncan an intense, probing look, "you better not break her heart."

Trevor slapped Duncan on the back. "I told you, dude. Obvious."

The three men walked away, leaving Duncan gaping at them.

"I would never break her heart," he muttered. He slipped Sera's badge into the pocket of his borrowed jacket. She'd need it back when they found her. "Because I love her, too."

"Undo her hands," Ramon instructed Mateo, while waving the gun he held at Sera. "We have to be on the move."

Mateo withdrew a lethal-looking knife from his back pocket. He slid the sharp edge across her face. She shrank back but kept her gaze locked with his. Anticipation of being free made her heart pound.

"Don't try anything," Ramon said. "I don't care if I return you missing an ear or a knee."

Curbing her urge to fight her way out, she stayed still as Mateo sliced the duct tape and released her hands.

She and Ivan were forced to walk out of the store-room into a large empty warehouse and out a side door to the green sedan. They shoved Ivan into the trunk and she was pushed into the back passenger seat with Mateo beside her, the knife a constant reminder of how precarious the situation.

As they drove away from the warehouse, she committed the location to memory. If she got out of her present situation alive, she wanted to be able to find Ramon's hideout. Though she wasn't sure he used the place for much since it was empty. But maybe the deed on the property would lead them to him.

They parked at a metered space on the street and left Ivan tied up in the trunk of the sedan.

Klyde Warren Park was a large public park in the heart of Dallas. It was a large, well-maintained lawn rimmed by decorated trees and small round tables and chairs that provided a gathering place. A beautiful pavilion at one end of the park offered shelter from the cold, or sun, depending on the weather. Stretching over five acres across the Woodall Rogers Freeway, the urban green space was used as a way to bring people together for festivities year-round.

On this afternoon, it was full of civilians, celebrating the Christmas season. Children ran around as their parents waited in line for pictures with Santa. Food carts lined one section of the park, providing a dizzying array of treats from savory to sweet. A Salvation Army Santa stood at the corner ringing his bell for donations.

The large, heavily decorated Christmas tree glistened in the sunlight. The colorful lights twinkled and the huge star on top was a clear symbol of the promise made on that amazing night two millenniums ago.

As she was escorted into the park, with Ramon walking slightly ahead and Mateo at her side, she witnessed Ramon acknowledge a man loitering at the edge of the park eating popcorn. She hadn't understood why he'd pick such a crowded place, but now the choice made sense. He had people already stationed at the park. She had no doubt Ramon would take innocent lives if he thought himself threatened.

Passing in front of the pavilion and heading toward the beautiful Christmas tree, Sera noticed a woman pushing a stroller had a slight bulge beneath her coat. A weapon. Was she undercover law enforcement or one of Ramon's plants? How would Sera know who was friend or foe?

This was going to go very badly. She sent up a prayer asking God to spare lives. And to let this exchange go without a hitch. They would have to get Ramon another way.

If the situation wasn't so dire, Sera would have enjoyed the park. But as she stood with Mateo's hand clamped around her left biceps and a gun jammed into her side, all she could think was how to protect the civilians. Her gaze tracked a woman chasing after a toddler. An elderly couple strolled hand in hand. A group of teenagers played a game of hacky sack.

All of them were oblivious to the danger invading the park.

As they rounded the Christmas tree, her heart thumped with both joy and heartache at the sight of Duncan standing near the back side of the tree near a lamppost with his hands deep inside the pockets of a dark jacket. A black beanie covered his head and ears. No doubt he had a communication link in one ear that would connect him to Trevor, and possibly Lucas and Brian.

There was no question in her mind that her fellow US marshals were close. Her brothers in arms. They always had her back. Just like Duncan. Her heart squeezed tight with love for this man.

What she'd said to him was true. It had been impulsive and maybe she'd let Ivan's pessimism get to her. But she'd wanted Duncan to know how she felt, just in case she didn't walk out of here alive.

"There's your guy," Ramon said.

With Mateo still gripping her left arm and Ramon on her right side, they approached Duncan. She tried to measure her steps, when all she wanted to do was run to his embrace. She steeled herself and channeled her energy. She would do whatever it took to make sure they both survived.

Duncan met her gaze, his blue eyes intense, the pupils large. She'd never seen his expression so full of angst. She'd put that look there. Was it possible he felt the same way about her? He hadn't been given a chance to respond because Ramon had hung up the phone. Would he have spurned her declaration? Or would he have welcomed her words?

"The flash drive," Ramon said, drawing Sera's focus.

Duncan removed one hand from his jacket and held up a silver flash drive. "Release her."

"Not so fast," Ramon said. "How do I know that's really the flash drive?"

Duncan frowned. "I'm not messing around with Sera's life. It's the flash drive."

"How do I know you didn't make a copy?" Ramon said.

Raising his eyebrows in his signature way, Duncan replied, "You don't. But what good will this flash drive do us. You've no doubt already moved your money."

Ramon grinned. "That I have. And yet, there's all that money sitting in those other accounts just waiting for someone to take them. It might as well be me. Certainly not that imbecile Ivan Pulanski."

Duncan extended his hand, offering the drive. "Do you want this or not?"

Ramon stepped forward, grasping Duncan by the hand and pulling him in close. "Oh, I want it. Do you really consider me fool enough not to anticipate that there are law enforcement crawling around like ants at a picnic? You and the deputy marshal are going to get us out of here."

"Ramon, that wasn't the deal," Sera said. "You have your own men here." She had to make sure the team was alerted to the danger so they could be extra careful.

"I'm making a new deal now," Ramon retorted. He shoved a gun into Duncan's rib cage. "Move it. Walk nice and easy out of the park. You see, your lady love here is correct—I have people in the park as well. If I give the signal, people will die. Women, children. You don't want that to happen, do you?"

Mateo spun Sera around and pushed her toward the closest exit of the park. They must have another ride waiting. Duncan and Ramon fell in step beside her.

"Why am I not surprised you wouldn't keep your

word?" Sera couldn't keep her disgust and anger from her voice.

Ramon's laugh grated across her skin like sandpaper. "I keep my word to those I love. I don't have any love for anyone in law enforcement."

At least he had some code of honor.

When they reached the street, Sera glimpsed Lucas around the corner of a silver pickup truck. There were still too many civilians milling about who could get hurt in the crossfire if this turned into a firefight. She turned to talk to Duncan. "Fall back."

Duncan scowled at her. "A little hard for me to do that right now."

She rolled her eyes, playing up her disgruntled act, even though she hoped he understood she meant their backup. "Why did you let him get so close to you?"

"Like you did any better." Raising his eyebrows, Duncan stopped walking and his voice dipped into surfer-dude mode, which loosened some of the tightness in her chest. He did get what she was doing, and this was his way of acknowledging the act.

"Getting yourself kidnapped from the hospital parking lot." He let out a scoff and stepped toward her but was yanked back by Ramon. "A real pro move, Deputy Marshal."

She grimaced at the truth in his words. She forced Mateo to stop so she could face Duncan. "None of this would be happening right now if you hadn't intervened. I had it handled. I work better alone. We're not partners."

He stepped closer, jerking away from Ramon, forcing the other man to let go of him. "None of this would be happening right now if your sister hadn't been in-volved with a criminal."

That was certainly true. She edged closer to Duncan, willing herself to keep from wrapping her arms around him. The danger was all too real and within striking distance. "But without your fancy moves we'd never get out of the situation."

A hint of a grin showed on his face despite the scowl darkening his eyes. "I can show you fancy moves, lady. Just you watch."

"Enough of this," Ramon said, stepping closer and grabbing Duncan again. "What are you two up to?"

Raising his eyebrow, Duncan said, "Mrs. Claus."

Dipping her chin in acknowledgement, she replied, "Santa."

Swiftly, Duncan shifted, ramming his good shoulder into Ramon and reaching for the gun. They struggled for possession of the weapon.

Sera didn't hesitate—she turned into Mateo, wrap-ping her hands around the SIG Saur and Mateo's hands, giving a sharp twist while driving her knee into his groin.

He doubled over, his grip on the gun going slack.

She knocked the weapon from his hand and it clat-tered to the ground. She bent to scoop it up.

He growled and lunged at her, his hands grasping her around the neck. His fingers dug into the soft flesh of her esophagus with painful intensity. She pummeled his arms. Her windpipe closed, cutting off her air.

There was a rush of footsteps as chaos erupted all around them. Ramon's men moved to intervene, meet-ing undercover officers. Then Lucas was there snaking an arm around Mateo's windpipe and giving him a knee to the kidneys. Mateo released his hold on her.

Gasping for breath, Sera twisted to see Ramon hitting Duncan in his wounded arm with the gun in his hand. Duncan fell to his knees while swinging his good fist to hit Ramon repeatedly in the thigh.

A roaring fury burst through Sera like Fourth of July pyrotechnics. She tackled Ramon, wrapping her arms around his legs, then lifted him off his feet and slammed him to the ground.

"Sera, no!" Duncan shouted.

Ramon rolled her over, his weight heavy. She planted her feet and lifted her hips to buck him off. The loud report of a gun assaulted her ears.

FIFTEEN

Sera shuddered as searing pain exploded in her thigh. Ramon was suddenly gone, his heavy weight no longer crushing her and stealing her breath. She stared at the overcast sky, panting through the agony of fire in her leg. She needed to get up, to move. She couldn't let Vega get away.

Strong arms slipped around her and lifted her off the ground. A wave of fear crashed over her. She struggled, trying to break loose.

"It's me." Duncan's gentle tone penetrated through the haze of pain and fear. "I've got you."

"No." She tried to push away from him even as she wanted to melt into his embrace. "You're injured. You shouldn't be carrying me."

"You've been shot." He shifted her closer. "We need to get you to an ambulance."

"Shot?" Of course. But still—she didn't want to hurt him. She never wanted to hurt him. "I can hobble."

"Always so stubborn," he murmured. "Just let me help you."

Repressing the urge to argue, she allowed Duncan

to carry her to a waiting ambulance bay. She laid her head against his chest. The Kevlar beneath her cheek kept her from hearing his heartbeat. His grip was sure. His hold on her secure. "Ivan is in the back of the green sedan parked at the other end of the park."

"I'll make sure he's released and taken into custody," he said.

"What about Angelina?" Sera hated to imagine her sister behind bars.

"I'll talk to the AG," Duncan assured her. "You concentrate on healing."

At the ambulance, he laid her on a gurney and helped load her into the back compartment. A paramedic slipped an oxygen mask over her face. Another paramedic put an IV needle in the back of her hand, attached to a bag of fluids.

"I can give you something for the pain," the paramedic said.

She shook her head. "Duncan?"

"Let them take care of you," he said as he stepped away.

The doors of the ambulance bay closed, blocking her view of Duncan, her view of her possible future.

With his heart in his throat, Duncan stared at the ambulance as it drove away. Sera had been shot. Hurt by Vega.

Hands fisted at his sides, he marched to where officers were about to place Vega into a cruiser.

"You'll pay for hurting her," Duncan said. "I'll make sure you never see the outside of a prison again."

Vega's sly smile made Duncan's teeth ache. "We'll see."

"We will," Duncan assured him. "There's no getting

out of this for you." Duncan stepped back to make room for the officers. "Get him out of here."

Duncan would do all in his power to make sure the charges against Vega stuck like glue.

Once Vega was locked inside the car, Duncan moved to where two officers were taking statements.

"There's a green sedan at the far end of the park," Duncan told them. "A suspect is locked in the trunk. He needs to be taken in and booked."

"On it." The officers hustled away.

A hand clamped down on Duncan's shoulder. He found himself facing Lucas and Brian.

"Why didn't you go with Sera to the hospital?" Brian asked. "She needs you."

"I—" Duncan faltered. Now that he'd made sure Vega was in custody, there was only one thought on his mind. Sera. "I'm headed there now if you'll drive."

At the hospital, Duncan was told Sera was in surgery to remove the bullet from her thigh. There was no reason to believe that she wouldn't come through the operation.

Yet, Duncan made his way to the hospital chapel, where he bowed his head and prayed.

The scent of a spring garden pulled Sera to consciousness. Her eyelids fluttered open. Memory rushed in. She'd been shot and taken by ambulance to the hospital. The last thing she remembered was the doctor telling her to count backward from ten. She was pretty sure she had only made it to eight.

Awareness settled in. Warmth covered her hand. She

turned her head to see Duncan. His hand engulfed hers, his chin rested on his chest and his eyes were closed.

Love bloomed within her like the array of flowers lined up along the edge of the windowsill.

She squeezed his hand. He sat up, his eyes opening and his gaze focusing on her.

"You're awake." His smooth-as-honey voice was so dear.

"Have you been here long?" she asked, her voice coming out like a croak.

Angelina stepped into view, putting her hand on Duncan's shoulder. "Ever since the surgery."

The pull of sleep was strong. Sera tried to fight it. "Vega?"

"In custody," Duncan assured her. "We don't have to worry about him anymore."

"Good." Her body felt heavy and light at the same time.

Duncan cupped her cheek. "Rest. We'll talk later."

A protest rose but fatigue and the drugs in her system made her tongue feel fat and lazy. She nodded and went back to sleep.

Two days later, Sera sat up in the hospital bed waiting for the doctor to come in and release her. The bullet had nicked her femur, but otherwise the damage was minimal. She would require six to eight weeks of rehab before the marshals service would consider her returning to work.

She intended to spend the time with her family. The plan was to recuperate at Camp Strong, the camp Victoria Armstrong ran for at-risk teens throughout the year, except at Christmastime. Victoria had a cabin ready for her and one for Angelina and Grace.

The call to their parents, reconnecting them to Angelina and letting them know they had a granddaughter, had been emotional and upsetting in many ways but was also good. Their mother promised to visit in the New Year and their father said he'd come in February.

Now that Ramon Vega and his crew had been arrested and were in jail awaiting their trial, they were all safe. At some point Sera would have to testify at Vega's trial. But that was down the line. Ivan Pulanski had also been arrested, though he intended to plead guilty to the pending charges of reckless endangerment and kidnapping. He would be going to prison.

Duncan had talked to the attorney general of Texas, as promised. The AG had taken into account that Angelina had given Sera the flash drive and had been acting under duress as an accomplice to Ivan and his shenanigans. She had been placed on probation and was scheduled to attend therapy sessions as well as do community service in the New Year.

All in all, everything was going well. Yet, Sera felt unsettled. She longed to see Duncan, but he hadn't returned since that first day after the surgery. She'd heard that the task force was busy writing up their after-action reports, something she would have to do once she was released from the hospital.

She didn't know when or if she'd see him again and the ache that thought caused was almost more than she could bear. She'd admitted her love to him. She didn't regret telling him, but she couldn't deny she was hurt that he hadn't at least acknowledged her confession. Why hadn't he visited again? Had he already left for another assignment?

Her gaze went to her sister, who was sitting in the corner flipping through a magazine. Her dark hair was clipped back and a pretty, red sweater complimented her complexion. Her sister was beautiful.

Grace sat in a chair facing the television with a holiday rom-com playing with the sound down low. She had on comfy sweats, and her dark hair was pulled back into a high ponytail. She looked so much like how Sera remembered Angelina as a teen.

Grace had finished her midterm exams with high marks. Since she was now on break, she'd decided she wanted to get to know her aunt. Which was just fine by Sera. They'd spent many hours talking and watching Christmas movies.

"Angie," Sera called to her sister.

Setting aside the magazine, Angelina was at Sera's side in an instant. "What can I do?"

Angelina had hardly left Sera's side. An unexpected surprise. Considering their past, Sera wouldn't have blinked if Angelina had bailed. But she hadn't. Holding out her hand, Sera waited for Angelina to take it. "I wanted to tell you—I do forgive you."

Tears welled in Angelina's eyes. She squeezed Sera's hand. "I'm glad. I'm never leaving you again."

"That would require you moving to San Antonio," Sera pointed out.

"Oh. Well, I mean metaphorically. We'll stay in touch and see each other often," Angelina amended. "It's only a four-hour drive. And in Texas time, that's nothing."

"True."

A knock sounded at the room door.

"Come in," Sera called out.

Duncan walked in and her heart stuttered. He was here.

In one hand, he carried a bouquet of beautiful gardenias with red carnations and greenery in a silver vase. Under his other arm, he carried a large red box with a gold bow. But what had her gaping was the fact that he was dressed once again as Santa Claus.

The red hat with the white pompom covered his brown hair, while tufts of white stuck out at the edges. His fake beard covered his strong jaw and his blue eyes twinkled beneath the fake bushy white eyebrows. The red velvet suit protruded around the middle and his black, knee-high boots clacked against the hospital's linoleum flooring.

"Ho, ho, ho," Duncan said with a smile. "Merry Christmas. Is there room on that shelf for another bouquet?"

Grace jumped up from the chair and hurried across the room to take the bouquet from Duncan. "There's always room for flowers. These are lovely."

Duncan approached the bed, his gaze searching her face. "How are you?"

"Me? I'm good. What are you doing? Why are you dressed as Santa?" She frowned with concern. "Are you going on another undercover assignment?"

He pulled up a chair. "No, this is just for fun." He laid the large red box next to her on the bed. "I told you I like to be of service at Christmas. I figured the current occupants of the hospital might need a little cheeriness."

He'd certainly cheered her up. Her heart pounded

in her chest. She wished she'd had Angelina brush her hair. "I'm being released today."

"I know," he said. "Two little birds told me."

"Oh, really?" Sera glanced at her sister and niece, who stood at the foot of the bed with wide-eyed innocence. "No one told me you were coming."

"I was hoping," Duncan said, drawing her attention. "Maybe you might like to join me in spreading some holiday cheer?"

Gesturing to her leg, she said, "I don't see how I could do that."

"Ever hear of a wheelchair?" He lifted the lid off the big box to reveal a replica of her Mrs. Claus disguise.

A laugh burst from her. "A hobbled Mrs. Claus."

"Nobody will blink an eye," he said. "The main thing is that we are together." He held out his hand. She placed hers within his grasp and their fingers entwined. Tentative hope gripped her insides. Together? What did he mean?

Duncan looked to Angelina and Grace. "Ladies, would you mind giving us the room?"

"Oh, um, of course not," Angelina sputtered. She urged Grace out of the hospital room door and shut it behind them.

"You just shooed away my dressing help," Sera said.

"They can come back in a minute," he said. "But you and I have unfinished business."

Her pulse fluttered and a nervous quiver raced over her limbs. "We do?"

"You made a declaration." His deliciously charming voice cascaded over her. "And I didn't get a chance to respond."

A spark of attraction and anticipation flared within her. "This is true." She shrugged, trying not to appear too eager. "An oversight on your part?"

Then, in a rush she said, "If not, you don't have to say anything. I didn't mean to put you on the spot. The situation was getting out of control. I let Ivan's pessimism rub off on me, so I—" She couldn't bring herself to say she didn't mean it. Because she had. She still did. She loved Duncan with all her heart.

After a beat of silence, he said, "Are you finished?"

She sighed, bracing herself to be let down. "Give it to me straight."

Better to rip off the Band-Aid than for her to agonize over whether there was a future for them or not.

He lifted her hand and turned it palm up. He bent to place a kiss in the center, his lips creating a warm glow that traveled up her arm.

"I have a declaration of my own," he murmured softly. "Seraphina Morales, I have fallen in love with you."

She let out a gasp of joy. "You have?"

"I have. You have taught me to take risks. And the value of loyalty. You've helped me see how determination and persistence pay off. I need my Mrs. Claus."

Heart melting, she squeezed his hand. "And you've taught me to be prepared and to ask for help. You've made me a better marshal. A better person."

He leaned in close, heat from his body enveloping her in a comforting cocoon. "May I kiss you now?"

She cocked an eyebrow and stared into his mesmerizing eyes. "You didn't ask for permission last time."

"I learn from my mistakes," he said. "Mrs. Claus, may I kiss you?"

Anticipation revved in her veins. "Please do."

He pressed his lips to hers, the fake beard tickling her skin. He cupped her face with his free hand while he brought their joined palms to his heart. The kiss was sweet and tender, and so thrilling.

When he eased away, she followed him until a twinge in her leg had her stilling. "Why did you stop?"

"We have people waiting on us." He lifted her knuckles to his lips and kissed them. "For now, you're Mrs. Claus. But one day, I hope that you will agree to be Mrs. O'Brien."

Her breath caught in her chest. Happiness spread over her like liquid fire. "I look forward to that day."

Eyes glimmering, he relinquished his hold on her and stood. He put his finger to his nose and winked. "Hurry up, Mrs. Claus. There are children waiting for their toys."

Grinning, she asked, "You have toys?"

"Of course. I didn't come empty-handed."

"No, you're always prepared and ready to do what's needed."

"Just remember that when we are old and resemble these characters a little bit too much." He patted the padded belly beneath his red jacket.

She lifted the gray wig from the box and shook it at him. "Go on, now. Send in my two elves."

His booming laugh wrapped around her heart, letting her know that their future, God willing, would be merry and bright.

* * * * *

If you liked this story from Terri Reed,
check out her previous
Love Inspired Suspense books,

Buried Mountain Secrets
Secret Mountain Hideout
Christmas Protection Detail
Secret Sabotage
Forced to Flee
Forced to Hide
Alaska K-9 Unit
Alaskan Rescue
Rocky Mountain K-9 Unit
Detection Detail
Pacific Northwest K-9 Unit
Explosive Trail

Available now from
Love Inspired Suspense!

Find more great reads at
www.LoveInspired.com.

Dear Reader,

Thank you for coming on this journey. I have wanted to tell Sera's story since she first appeared in Forced to Flee and again in Forced to Hide. She's a tough lady who can hold her own in any situation. But when she finds herself falling for the handsome DEA agent, she's flummoxed. Having a romantic relationship wasn't on her agenda. Neither was finding her long-lost sister. It was fun to throw obstacles up for Sera to deal with. And Duncan was the perfect foil, both charming and driven. Together they made a good team. It just took them a while to come to that conclusion. These two characters are very dear to my heart, as is the verse at the opening of the book. The Psalms have a touch of drama, and this verse is no exception. When you read different translations of this verse, you get a better understanding of how the poem speaks to the passion of writing for God. And this, my friend, is my passion. Writing to bless God and to bless you with my stories. I hope that this holiday season you are blessed beyond measure. I'd be blessed if you stopped in at my webpage, https://www.terrireed.com, and signed up for my newsletter. I love to do giveaways and share what's going on in my life.

Until we meet again,
Terri Reed

COMING NEXT MONTH FROM

COMING NEXT MONTH FROM
Love Inspired Suspense

TRACKING STOLEN TREASURES
K-9 Search and Rescue • by Lisa Phillips
On the trail of a vicious jewel-theft ring, FBI special agent
Alena Sanchez is undercover at a medical conference when her
prime suspect is kidnapped. Now she'll have to team up with K-9
officer Hank Miller to uncover how theft leads to cold-blooded murder.

BURIED GRAVE SECRETS
Crisis Rescue Team • by Darlene L. Turner
When forensic anthropologist Jordyn Miller is targeted for discovering
an unmarked graveyard, she knows someone is determined to keep
old secrets buried. Constable Colt Peters and his K-9 protector dog
are called in to guard her life—but exposing a serial killer could be the
last thing they do...

UNDERCOVER BABY RESCUE
by Maggie K. Black
To save his stolen nephew from a dangerous trafficking organization,
Officer Justin Leacock will have to go undercover as a married couple
with his former fiancée, Detective Violet Jones. But finding the boy
isn't enough—they must outwit the kidnappers on their tail and
survive the ruthless icy wilderness, too...

MONTANA WITNESS CHASE
by Sharon Dunn
After testifying against her brother's murderer, Hope Miller is placed in
witness protection—only to be attacked at her new safe house. With her
identity compromised, it's up to US marshal Andrew Lewis to safeguard
her. But stopping the crime ring could prove lethal for them both.

DANGEROUS RANCH THREAT
by Karen Kirst
When rancher Cassie West discovers that several murder victims bear
a striking resemblance to her, it's clear there's a serial killer at large...
and she's the next target. Can she and her temporary ranch hand
Luke McCoy expose the killer before they exact vengeance?

HUNTED IN THE MOUNTAINS
by Addie Ellis
Pursued by assailants, a terrified child shows up at Julia Fay's door—
and soon they're both running for their lives. Can Julia and former
navy SEAL Troy Walker protect the boy against the unknown...when
the truth could get them killed?

———————

**LOOK FOR THESE AND OTHER LOVE INSPIRED BOOKS WHEREVER
BOOKS ARE SOLD, INCLUDING MOST BOOKSTORES, SUPERMARKETS,
DISCOUNT STORES AND DRUGSTORES.**

LISCNM1123

Get 3 FREE REWARDS!

We'll send you 2 FREE Books plus a FREE Mystery Gift.

FREE Value Over **$20**

Both the **Love Inspired®** and **Love Inspired®** Suspense series feature compelling novels filled with inspirational romance, faith, forgiveness and hope.

YES! Please send me 2 FREE novels from the Love Inspired or Love Inspired Suspense series and my FREE gift (gift is worth about $10 retail). After receiving them, if I don't wish to receive any more books, I can return the shipping statement marked "cancel." If I don't cancel, I will receive 6 brand-new Love Inspired Larger-Print books or Love Inspired Suspense Larger-Print books every month and be billed just $6.49 each in the U.S. or $6.74 each in Canada. That is a savings of at least 16% off the cover price. It's quite a bargain! Shipping and handling is just 50¢ per book in the U.S. and $1.25 per book in Canada.* I understand that accepting the 2 free books and gift places me under no obligation to buy anything. I can always return a shipment and cancel at any time by calling the number below. The free books and gift are mine to keep no matter what I decide.

Choose one:
- ☐ **Love Inspired Larger-Print** (122/322 BPA GRPA)
- ☐ **Love Inspired Suspense Larger-Print** (107/307 BPA GRPA)
- ☐ **Or Try Both!** (122/322 & 107/307 BPA GRRP)

Name (please print)

Address   Apt. #

City   State/Province   Zip/Postal Code

Email: Please check this box ☐ if you would like to receive newsletters and promotional emails from Harlequin Enterprises ULC and its affiliates. You can unsubscribe anytime.

Mail to the **Harlequin Reader Service:**
IN U.S.A.: P.O. Box 1341, Buffalo, NY 14240-8531
IN CANADA: P.O. Box 603, Fort Erie, Ontario L2A 5X3

Want to try 2 free books from another series! Call 1-800-873-8635 or visit www.ReaderService.com.

*Terms and prices subject to change without notice. Prices do not include sales taxes, which will be charged (if applicable) based on your state or country of residence. Canadian residents will be charged applicable taxes. Offer not valid in Quebec. This offer is limited to one order per household. Books received may not be as shown. Not valid for current subscribers to the Love Inspired or Love Inspired Suspense series. All orders subject to approval. Credit or debit balances in a customer's account(s) may be offset by any other outstanding balance owed by or to the customer. Please allow 4 to 6 weeks for delivery. Offer available while quantities last.

Your Privacy—Your information is being collected by Harlequin Enterprises ULC, operating as Harlequin Reader Service. For a complete summary of the information we collect, how we use this information and to whom it is disclosed, please visit our privacy notice located at corporate.harlequin.com/privacy-notice. From time to time we may also exchange your personal information with reputable third parties. If you wish to opt out of this sharing of your personal information, please visit readerservice.com/consumerschoice or call 1-800-873-8635. **Notice to California Residents**—Under California law, you have specific rights to control and access your data. For more information on these rights and how to exercise them, visit corporate.harlequin.com/california-privacy.

LIRLIS23

HARLEQUIN
PLUS

Try the best multimedia subscription service for romance readers like you!

Read, Watch and Play.

Experience the easiest way to get the romance content you crave.

Start your **FREE TRIAL** at
<u>www.harlequinplus.com/freetrial</u>.